TERMINATION ORDER

ALSO BY BRENT TOWNS

Fear the Reaper Series

The Gods of War Series

The MI6 Files

Talon Series

Mark Hayes Series

Dave Nash Thrillers

Treasure Series

TERMINATION ORDER

A TEAM REAPER THRILLER
BOOK 3

BRENT TOWNS

ROUGH
EDGES
PRESS

FROM THE CENTRAL
INTELLIGENCE AGENCY WORLD
FACT BOOK:

United States: *World's largest consumer of cocaine (shipped from Colombia through Mexico and the Caribbean), Colombian heroin, and Mexican heroin and marijuana; major consumer of ecstasy and Mexican methamphetamine.*
Latvia: *Transshipment and destination point for cocaine, synthetic drugs, opiates, and cannabis from Southwest Asia, Western Europe, Latin America, and neighboring Baltic countries*
Poland: *A major illicit producer of synthetic drugs for the international market; minor transshipment point for Southwest Asian heroin and Latin American cocaine to Western Europe.*

TERMINATION ORDER

CHAPTER 1

HELL TOWN, MOJAVE DESERT

KANE WAS in a whole world of hurt. So much so, he was already bleeding. Grinder stepped back from him and asked the question again. "Is your name John Kane? Are you some kind of law?"

"Are you going to keep pushing this guy's fist around with your face, Reaper, or do you want me to fix the issue?" Axel 'Axe' Burton's voice rang in Kane's ear.

John 'Reaper' Kane, ex-recon marine, 6-foot-4 of solid muscle, broad shoulders, and black hair, ignored the question. Instead, he stared at the biker gang leader and smiled, exposing blood-stained teeth. "Hi, have we met before?"

Grinder's fist lashed out again, delivering a solid blow. "We can do this, one of two ways, pig. Guess which way this is?"

Kane had been undercover for two months with the biker gang known as The Devils. The Worldwide Drug Initiative, the name for those he worked for and with, had been trying to put Grinder's bastards out of business since a request for assistance had come in from the DEA. Hell Town was their town. A place of streets lined with rundown buildings made from adobe and wood. A burning furnace out in the desert where their word was law.

So far, the mission had been all about gathering intelligence on suppliers and distributors, but it had quickly turned to being about life and death.

The Devils trafficked in drugs, women, and firearms. They also had known links to the cartels in Mexico and the Russian Mafia. But they didn't work for them; they dealt with them. The Devils were a breed of their own, vicious and brutal in their dealings, and they backed away from no one.

After several months, Kane had finally been accepted into the untrusting society. He'd gotten tattoos, albeit fake, except for the one of the Grim Reaper on his back, beaten people so bad they were hospitalized, ran drugs interstate, and been involved in an armored car heist in Utah. He'd put his life on the line for his team, and now he needed them.

He was surrounded. Thirty foul-smelling, hairy assed, tattooed thugs led by a large gorilla of a man everyone called Grinder. He too was covered in tattoos and had a large, dirty beard which hung down his chest.

Kane had somehow been betrayed. Unable to work out by whom or why, he only knew that someone had told Grinder about him.

Grinder hit him again, and he staggered across the tight circle to be grabbed by Tiny. The man mountain punched him in the face, and Kane's head swam.

Blood flowed freely from several points on his face, including a cut above his left eye, one on his cheek, a split lip, and he was sure his nose was broken.

He lurched to the right and came face to face with a toothless moll.

She kneed Kane in his balls, and he dropped to the pavement and threw up.

Reaper clawed his way to his feet and swayed as he tried to steady himself. Looking about him at all the menacing faces, his stare fell on Iona.

He'd shared her bed many times over the past couple of months. Now the blonde-haired, lithe-bodied woman with the ice-blue eyes looked like the rest of them.

A rough-looking biker with the handle Wrench stepped forward. "Let me do it, Grinder. I been wanting to cap this fucker for a long time."

You didn't have to be a rocket scientist to work out why. Due to the fact that Kane had been screwing Iona, and Wrench had been passed over for him, his ego had taken a massive hit.

Grinder looked thoughtfully at him and nodded. "All right. Do it."

Wrench smiled, and the scar on the left side of his face puckered. Stepping forward, eager to get rid of his main rival for Iona's affections, he reached behind his back and drew an FN Five-Seven handgun. Raising it in a massive paw, he placed the black weapon against Kane's forehead.

The condemned man raised his right hand and said, "Wait. Hold on. Tell me how you knew."

"Does it matter?" Grinder asked from behind him.

"It does to me."

Grinder shrugged.

"Who?"

"No, sir. You don't get to know. Kill him, Wrench."

Wrench gave Kane a mirthless smile. "With pleasure."

The biker's finger started to tighten on the trigger when a sound from further along the pot-holed street reached their ears. Kane looked around Grinder and saw a red Jeep Wrangler coming towards them. It stopped, and two women stood up on the front seats, revealing short shorts and bikini tops. The driver, an athletically-built woman in her early forties with dark hair, gave them all a huge smile. She said, "Hi, guys, want to party?"

———

A trickle of sweat rolled down Kane's right cheek as he waited for Wrench to pull the trigger. It mixed with the partially-dried blood and formed a pale pink rivulet which continued down the side of his neck.

"Who the fuck are you?" Grinder snarled.

"I can make all your dreams come true, Sugar," Mary Thurston told him seductively. "Both me and my friend."

Had anyone moved around behind the Jeep, they might have had more reason for concern than they showed. For tucked in the back of the women's cut-off shorts were two Sig Sauer M17 handguns.

Axe's voice filled Kane's ear, the opposite one to which Wrench had his FN pointed. "Just so you know, good buddy, Carlos and Brick are at the south end of town in a DPV."

"The gang's all here," Kane murmured.

"What did you say, shithead?" Wrench growled, dragging his gaze away from the eye candy that had just driven into town. He rapped the weapon in his hand over Kane's head in a painful blow.

"Just say the word, Reaper, and I'll put a 7.62 slug in the fucker's head," Axe said without taking his eye from the scope atop the M110 Semi-Automatic Sniper System.

"What's going on?" Grinder growled, taking his attention away from Thurston and Cara.

"Nothing," Wrench assured him. "Just a friendly chat."

"What did he do?" Cara asked.

Grinder turned and stared at her. Cara Billings was in her mid-thirties. She was slim but not thin, her body was that of a professional trainer, toned. Her hair was dark, face tanned like the rest of her, and she wore aviator sunglasses. In her life, she'd been a marine lieutenant and a deputy sheriff. Right now, she was second in charge of a field team designated 'Team Reaper'. The lady beside her, an ex-ranger, also a general in the U.S. military, was the overall commander of both teams 'Reaper' and 'Bravo'.

"What he did don't concern you, missy," Grinder snapped. "So, how about you both just turn around and get the hell out of here."

They stared at each other in silence. The uncanny way these women seemed so calm actually unnerved the Devil's leader.

"I have a creeper at the back of the crowd," Axe's voice came over comms. "He looks to be carrying an MP7."

"Where do they get these damned weapons from?" Ferrero asked no one in particular, talking about the German made Heckler and Koch *Maschinenpistole 7*.

"Hey, boss, you're back online," Axe observed.

Luis Ferrero, former DEA agent, now in charge of operations under Thurston, along with Brooke Reynolds, Pete Teller, and Sam Swift, were in a secure location in Los Angeles where the team had been based out of since the commencement of the operation. He was in his late forties with graying hair, and solidly built.

"Not sure for how long, Reaper Three. Bravo, our electronics are still playing up, so we expect to lose comms again soon. I've dispatched a Black Hawk to assist. ETA ten minutes."

Thurston knew five minutes was too late, let alone ten. This shit was going down now whether they liked it or not. She whispered, "Reaper, call it when you're ready."

"Check that," Axe said again. "I now have four other tangos with a mix of Mac-11s and what looks to be M4s. They are all at the back of the crowd."

Kane knew he was in a bad spot. And there was every chance that he could die before the situation played out. But he was damned if it was going to be without a fight. "Axe, I've had enough of this shit."

"Copy. Sending."

Axe squeezed the trigger on the M110, and it slammed back into his shoulder. The shot was perhaps seven-hundred meters, give or take. The 7.62mm bullet exploded from the barrel at seven-hundred and eighty-three meters per second. Which meant it took just under that second of flight time before punching into the biker's skull, the man dropping the MP7 he was packing.

The distraction was all Kane needed to save his life, and he took full advantage.

Wrench's reaction was quick and automatic. He heard the gunshot and swung his head toward the noise.

Kane moved with blinding speed. Bringing his hands up, he grabbed Wrench's Five-Seven and twisted with savage intent. Hearing the wrist bones give, and the biker cry out in pain, Kane felt the man loosen his grasp on the gun, and he pulled the weapon free. Reversing it, he changed it over to his right hand and pulled the trigger.

The bullet punched into Wrench's skull just between and slightly above his two surprised, wide eyes, and his head snapped back. The .224 caliber round blew out the back in a bright spray of blood, gore, and bone, coating the toothless moll's face and chest in the ghastly substance. She screamed in disgust and wiped it from her eyes.

Without hesitation, Kane swiveled and brought the weapon into line with Grinder who'd turned at the sound of the first shot. BLAM! BLAM! Two in his barrel chest and the Devil's leader was down and bleeding out.

For a big man, Tiny was agile and moved fast. Before Kane knew it and could turn to face the big man's advance, he was too slow, and the man was upon him, strong hands wrapping around his throat in a vice-like grip, lifting him from the pavement. Then came the crushing pressure which threatened to cut off his air.

Bright lights flashed in front of his eyes, and his face turned purple. Kane drove the Five-Seven into the big biker's middle and squeezed the trigger three times. BLAM! BLAM! BLAM!

Tiny released him and staggered back, pressing his hands to his own bloodied middle and then raising them in front of his face. Horrified and disbelieving the sight of the blood- covered appendages, he returned his gaze to his shooter, and a howl of rage escaped his throat as he lumbered forward.

Still gasping for breath, Kane wasn't in the best position to ward off the renewed and frenzied attack. The Five-Seven started to come up. The big man reached out with bloody hands to finish what he'd started.

BLAM!

A third eye appeared above the bridge of his nose as the slug did its job, and Tiny dropped like a stone.

Kane turned and stared gratefully at Thurston who was standing in the back of the Jeep, M17 drawn and level from where she'd fired.

Suddenly, Hoover burst from the stunned crowd, a knife held above her still blood-spattered head and shoulders, the blade flickering in the sunlight. She screeched. High-pitched, chilling.

BLAM!

Cut short.

Kane had one shot left. He thought. Maybe.

Turning in a circle, the gun moved with him. "Which one of you pricks is next?" he asked, his voice thick through his battered lips. He spit on the street.

Settling his gaze on Iona, she smiled at him, seemingly impressed by what she'd just seen. She disappeared from the crowd.

"Reaper!" Cara shouted. He turned and saw the HK416 sailing through the air toward him. He dropped the FN and deftly caught the carbine then brought it around and saw an ugly biker with a MAC-11, pushing through to the front of the crowd.

Kane squeezed the trigger, and the 416 roared. Because the fire selector was set to semi-auto, it only fired once. The 5.56mm bullet hammered into the biker's chest, spinning him around.

His brain's final impulse sent a signal to his right-hand trigger finger which tightened on the MAC-11's trigger and held it all the way back. The weapon burned through the thirty-round magazine in a heartbeat, every one of its .380 ACP slugs flying wildly through the air. Most failed to find flesh, however, some didn't. One female biker went down with lead in her throat and lay there gurgling in her own dark, thick blood. Two stitched across the naked chest of a biker called T-Rex, while another smashed into the center of Vomit's face, turning the ugly façade into a gruesome mush.

Kane lurched forward in a shuffling run and found shelter behind the Jeep with Thurston and Cara. The latter stared at him and said, "You look like shit."

"I don't feel much better."

Axe's voice came over the comms with its usual calm-under-fire tone. "Guys, we may have a problem. I can see four black SUVs coming in from the west."

There was a crack from the M110, and then Axe said, "Make that five. I say again, there are five SUVs coming in from the west."

Thurston's handgun barked, and a shot intended for a biker missed and caused the would-be shooter to duck and run for cover. She cursed under her breath and then said, "Do you have eyes on, Zero?"

"Wait one, Bravo."

Thurston and Cara had both discarded their M17s and were using HK416s. The general's second shot didn't miss her target, and a large tattooed man with an FN Five-Seven was kicked sideways and sprawled onto the asphalt.

Bullets spanged off the Jeep's exterior and ricocheted away.

With a loud roar, the DPV (Desert Patrol Vehicle) emerged from a side street. Carlos Arenas, ex-Mexican special forces commander was behind the wheel. In the passenger seat was Richard 'Brick' Peters. He was the team's combat medic. An ex-SEAL, Brick had come on board after his security team had been ambushed in Mexico while escorting the U.S. Ambassador to an opening ceremony, and most of them getting killed by cartel soldiers. He was a big man with a shaved head and tattoos on his arms.

In Brick's hands was an M249 Light Machinegun. No sooner had the DPV skidded to a stop, the M249 rattled to life. Armed bikers jerked and fell with multiple gunshot wounds. Arenas came clear of the vehicle and opened up on a biker with an M4 pointed in the direction of the Jeep. The man dropped and went still, three fast rounds from the 416 had stopped him cold.

And suddenly it was over. Those of The Devils who weren't dead had scattered, their hierarchy cut down. Their town fortress conquered by a much smaller force.

"Bravo, our friends have arrived," Axe warned. "I don't like the look of this."

"Zero," said Thurston. "Have you got anything?"

"If I had to guess, Bravo," Ferrero said, "I'd say CIA."

Thurston frowned. "What the..."

The five black SUVs stormed into the small town's main street. They stopped just short of the battle zone in a V formation and disgorged fifteen men all dressed in black and wearing tactical gear. Except for one man. He wore a suit and dark glasses.

"Talk about men in fucking black," Axe growled over the comms.

"Keep an eye on them, Axe," Kane said in a low voice.

Thurston said, "How far out is that Black Hawk, Luis?"

"Five minutes."

The man in the suit walked toward them, weaving through the dead on the ground. Beside him came a fair-haired man with broad shoulders and wearing polarized sunglasses. They stopped just short of where the team members stood.

"You people have been busy," he said in a gravelly voice.

Thurston stared at his square-jawed, clean-shaven face. She put him in his early forties. The man beside him was possibly ten years younger. Looking back at the man in the suit, she asked, "Who are you?"

The man smiled. "Let's just call me Smith, shall we? And you are?"

"General Mary Thurston," Thurston said but figured that whoever he was, he already knew that.

"Well, well," Smith said in a condescending tone. "You seem to be out of uniform, General."

"What are you doing here?"

Smith glanced at the man beside him and nodded. He turned back and said, "We have a little business here, and then we'll be gone."

The man at his side waved back at the men still with the SUVs, and five of them broke off. They ran toward a rundown building and disappeared inside.

"What business would that be?" Thurston asked.

Smith gave her a weak smile and looked up at the sky. "Very hot today isn't it. Personally, I dislike the heat. I can't for the life of me figure out why anyone would live in a godforsaken hole like this."

"Gotcha," Ferrero's voice came over the comms. "We'll see if we can put a name to the face for you."

There was a scuffle at the building that the five armed men had entered and now reappeared – with two others. Kane saw immediately that one of them was Iona! The other he'd never seen before. But regardless of the man's identity, he wasn't about to go quietly.

He managed to break away from his captors and ran toward the team. The men in black began to chase him, but the bulk of their gear slowed them down.

"Help me!" he cried out. "You must help me!"

A look of disgust combined with a touch with inconvenience descended over Smith's face. He reached inside his coat and took out a Sig Sauer P320. He pivoted at the waist and brought the weapon into line.

A flat crack sounded, and the running man's head snapped back, blood spraying from the exit wound. The prisoner dropped to the ground and didn't move.

"Shit!" Kane gasped and brought up his 416. The rest of the team did likewise, and soon there were weapons pointed in all directions. Except for Kane's. His was pointed at Smith's head.

"What the fuck was that?" he snarled.

"That was nothing to do with you, Mr. Kane."

"You know who I am?" Kane was stunned.

Smith smiled. "Of course."

Kane looked over the killer's shoulder at Iona, and the dime dropped. "She's one of yours."

"Who?"

"Iona."

Smith shrugged. "I think you need some medical attention. You look like you've been knocked around a bit."

The arrogance of the man was plain to see, and that pissed Kane off more than the realization of what had happened. But not by much. "You bastard! You had her tip them off to who I was. We were involved in something that wasn't to your liking, and you fucking had her tip them off!"

"What is the CIA doing operating an illegal op on U.S. soil, Mr. Smith?" Thurston asked.

"Who said we're CIA? As you said, that would be illegal."

"Asshole," Kane hissed and started forward, his battered face a mask of pain. He dropped the 416 on his approach. Smith's arrogance expected him to stop, but he didn't. By the time the CIA man realized his mistake, it was too late.

Smith tried to bring his weapon into play, but Kane was too quick for him. The P320 never even made it halfway before Kane closed his hand over the man's wrist and disarmed him. Then Kane used all of his unarmed combat experience, turning Smith around and wrapping his left arm around the man's throat. In his right hand, the Sig was pointed at the CIA man's nearest operator.

"Try it, and I'll put a bullet in your head," Kane warned him.

"Reaper!" Thurston cautioned him. "Let the nasty man go."

"Sorry, ma'am, he tried to get me killed. I can't let that slide."

Suddenly Ferrero came back over the comms. "Bravo, Slick was able to get a name for our friend. He's Mark Newcomb, CIA. Well known as a cleaner for the CIA Special Activities Division abroad."

Thurston knew what cleaner meant. Somehow the CIA had an op running here which had gone wrong, and Newcomb was here to tidy up the mess. But their op had gotten in the way. Thurston stared at the body on the ground and wondered how much of it was to do with him. She raised her gaze. "Kane, let Mr. Newcomb go. That's an order."

Kane released Newcomb, and a glance passed between the CIA man and his operator. Reaper handed the Sig back to him and said, "You should be more careful."

"So should you."

"Cara," Thurston said, "get a picture of our friend on the ground there."

She started forward, and Smith said, "I don't think so."

Cara stopped when he blocked her path.

"I'd move if I was you, Newcomb," Thurston snapped, running out of patience. "I have an outside shooter who can blow a tick off a dog's ass at one-thousand meters. I give him the word, and you're done."

Suddenly, a Black Hawk screamed overhead causing

everyone to look up. As it moved away, the sound of its rotor lowering, Thurston shouted, "That's ours too."

Knowing he was outgunned, Newcomb stepped aside, and Cara used her cell to take a picture. She tapped the keys and said, "Slick, on its way."

Newcomb stared at Thurston and asked, "Are we done here?"

"I think so."

Without another word, Newcomb and his man turned, starting back toward the SUVs. The CIA black ops operator said, "The boss ain't going to like this. We were meant to get rid of Hafeez quietly."

Without looking at the man, Newcomb said, "What does it matter now? Hafeez is gone. So are any of his CIA secrets."

Kane watched Iona as she climbed into an SUV along with Newcomb. Then all five vehicles started and turned around, leaving Hell Town behind them.

After they'd gone, Thurston said, "All right, let's start checking to see who's still alive. Kane, did you know this guy was here?"

"No, ma'am. I had no idea."

CHAPTER 2

TEAM REAPER HQ, EL PASO TEXAS—THREE DAYS LATER

THE PHONE on Thurston's desk rang twice before she picked it up. Placing it to her ear, she said, "Thurston."

"Mary, it's Hank," the voice of General Hank Jones came down the line. "There's not much time so just listen."

"Sir."

"You're about to get a visit from some very bad people. Just give them what they want, and they'll leave. My hands are tied on this one. The orders have come from over my head."

Concerned, Thurston asked, "Who are they, sir?"

"Newcomb and a handful of contractors that the CIA Special Activities Division use."

"Shit. Is this about what happened the other day, General?"

"Yes."

"What the hell did we stumble upon, sir?"

"I can't say, but you can be sure that it is bad because they're going to a lot of trouble to cover it up. Be careful, Mary, these people make other people disappear."

"We can handle them, General."

"I'm sure you can, just give them what they want, and they'll be gone."

"How long do I have?"

"Maybe ten minutes."

"Thank you, sir."

Thurston hung up and rose from her chair. Walking out of her office, she went to find Ferrero. It was in the briefing room that she found both him and Kane.

Ferrero was ex-DEA. He'd worked with Kane back in the day when the Drug Enforcement Administration was running covert ops in Colombia. In his late forties, Ferrero's hair was graying all over, and he was single and solidly built.

"We've got a problem. Where's Slick?"

"In operations," Ferrero said. "Why?"

"Follow me."

They hurried out to the operations room and found Swift at his computer. The computer tech had red hair and was thin built. He often bragged that there was nothing with a computer he couldn't do.

"Slick, bring up the external cameras," Thurston snapped.

The big screen came alive and showed the approach to the Team Reaper HQ. The parking lot was empty. "That's something," Thurston breathed. "All right. Everything you have on the search you were doing into our friends, back it up and store it somewhere. Separately."

"Yes, ma'am."

"You've got about eight minutes."

"What's going on, Mary?" Ferrero asked.

"I just received a call from Hank Jones. It would seem that our friend Newcomb and some of his hired help are coming here to seize whatever we have from the other day. The general has ordered me to cooperate with them. The whole thing is coming from higher up the chain."

"How high?" Kane asked.

"One would guess all the way to the top."

"Which means that it's something bad."

"Yes."

"You could say that," Swift said.

All three stared at him.

"What do you know?" Thurston asked.

"I was just about to come and find you when you found me," Swift explained. "Our friend, who was shot out in the desert, was a Pakistani journalist. Hafeez Jiskani."

An image flashed up on the second big screen of the dead man from Hell Town. Swift continued. "He's been making noise about a UAV strike last year in Pakistan. He claims that the strike against a Taliban training camp went wrong and a school was hit. Killed thirty school children. Both governments denied it, but I found this after some deep digging."

A grainy video flashed up onto the screen. There was an audio file with it, and someone was speaking in the background while the camera was panning around. A small body came into view, then another, and another. All the while the voice in the background was talking.

"Is that our friend Jiskani talking in the background?" Kane asked.

"Yes. It would seem he was right about the air strike," Swift said.

"Shit!" Thurston hissed. "Then what was he doing hanging out with The Devils?"

"They have contacts," Kane pointed out. "They must have got him into the country. Somehow, the CIA got wind of it. They weren't sure when, so they put Iona or whatever the fuck her name is, undercover in there to wait for Jiskani to show."

"It still doesn't explain why he was in the U.S.," Thurston said.

"Could you imagine if this got out?" Swift said. "We're in an election year. It sure would kill a candidate's run for office."

"I can't imagine the president sanctioning this, though."

"Someone wanted him dead," Kane pointed out.

"Put it on a thumb drive and hide it," Thurston ordered. "I'll talk to the general about it later. For now, we sit on it. What do we know about Newcomb? Apart from him being a CIA cleaner."

Swift said, "He takes his orders from the deputy director of the CIA who runs the Special Activities division personally."

"Paul Horn?" Thurston asked.

"Yes, ma'am. Apparently, he was a warrior from deep within the CIA covert ops. Anyway, Newcomb always hires outside people for his teams. The other day when you saw him, he was working with a team from Black Shield."

"The defense contractor?"

"Yes. They're in the middle of some negotiations with Poland and the U.S. Government at the moment for a missile defense system worth billions. Who also just happens to be one of the biggest donors to the president's campaign for reelection."

"And there it is," said Kane.

"There what is?" Thurston asked curiously.

"The reason why our journalist was killed. If that footage along with proof got out, Carter is screwed, doesn't get back in office, and Black Shield loses any chance of getting the missile contract. We all know what the other side of politics thinks of them."

"You think they would do that?"

"They're coming here for some reason," Kane pointed out.

"No," Swift said, "they're here."

They stared at the screen and watched as two SUVs pulled up. Doors opened, and eight people exited. One of which, Kane knew really well. "Iona."

They strode through the front door as though they owned the place. Arrogance seemed to ooze from every pore of their skin. And they even came armed with M4s. Stopping in the middle of the operations room, they looked around, ignoring the team's presence. What surprised Thurston the most was that Newcomb hadn't come alone. He'd brought another suit with him. This one had a lot more influence than most others. He was a thickset man with wavy hair and a square jaw. His name was Paul Horn.

"What can I do for you, Paul?" Thurston asked him.

Still, he ignored her and pointed to where Swift sat at his computer. "There. Start there."

An armed contractor walked over to where Swift sat and said, "Move away from the computer, sir."

Swift glanced at Thurston who nodded. He did as asked, and the contractor slung his M4 and leaned down below Swift's desk and pulled all wires from his hard drive and took the whole thing.

"Hey!" called Axe who'd suddenly appeared in the

doorway with Cara. "What the fuck do you think you're doing?"

"Stand down, Axe," Kane snapped. The tall ex-recon marine's eyes blazed.

Axe's gaze settled on Newcomb. "Oh, it's this mother-fucker again. Come to shit in our nest, have you?"

"Who are you?" Horn snapped at Axe.

"None of your damned business," Axe snapped back.

Horn turned away, his face red. He pointed at two more men. "Requisition anything you think is relevant."

"Just what the hell are you looking for, Horn?" Thurston growled as she ran out of patience.

"Anything we deem necessary to take, Mary."

Kane stared at Iona. He couldn't help himself and asked, "What's your name? Your real name?"

"You don't need to know that, Mr. Kane," Horn assured him.

"Uh, huh," Kane said. Then to Horn, "Are you the prick who ordered me burned?"

"And if I was?"

"Then you're an asshole. It almost got me killed."

Horn gave Kane a disinterested stare and turned to Thurston. "Tell your people to pull their heads in, Mary. I'm growing bored with their whining."

"Why'd you send your boys after the journalist? I'm sure it wasn't to kill him."

"Kane!" Thurston barked. "Let it go."

But the damage was already done. Horn's gaze grew hard, and he spoke in a threatening tone, "You'd do best to forget everything you saw out there. It has nothing to do with the likes of you."

Thurston knew Kane would keep pressing if she didn't intervene, and she caught Cara's eye. Cara hurried across to Kane and took his arm. "Come on, Reaper. Time to get out of the sandpit."

"I was only just getting started."

"And now you're finished."

Kane allowed Cara to lead him from the operations room. Once outside, Kane hissed, "I'd like to put a slug in that bastard's head."

"I'm sure the general would too, but obviously there's more in play here than I know about. Care to tell me?"

Kane filled her in on what he knew. Cara was stunned. "Wow."

"That's one way of putting it."

Horn and his men finished what they were doing and started to leave the building. Outside, Kane and Cara were standing, talking. As they walked past, Horn turned to him and said, "I'll remember you, Kane."

Reaper smiled coldly. "Be aware of this, Horn. I come across any of your men down range, and I see something like that again, I'll put them down, Horn. Understand?"

"Big talk for a little man, Kane," Horn said arrogantly.

"I guess we'll find out, won't we?"

Horn climbed into one of the SUVs with Newcomb and Iona, whose real name was Nicole Cresswell. Newcomb said, "He's trouble."

Horn nodded. "I feel we may have to kill that man someday."

―――――

By the time the CIA had finished, the operations room was a mess. When Kane and Cara walked back inside, the team was already starting to tidy up. Thurston caught sight of him and said, "Mr. Kane, a word."

Out of the corner of her mouth, Cara said, "Time to get spanked, Reaper."

Kane joined his commanding officer off to one side of the room. He could tell by the look in her eyes that she wasn't happy and she let him know. "What the fuck was that?" she hissed.

"I'm sorry…"

"I don't give a shit what you are. I expect better from my commanders on this team."

"Yes, ma'am."

"You let Horn know that we know about the journalist, which will have him wondering what else we know about what went down. And on top of that, if whoever is pulling the strings on this one thinks we know more than what we should, then *you* just made us targets as well. There is a time and place for anger, Kane, and that was not *it*!"

"Yes, ma'am."

"Help the others get tidied up."

"Ma'am."

Kane walked off, and Ferrero filled his void. "Is everything OK, Mary?"

"It will be," she said abruptly. "Listen, Luis, take over. I'm going to Washington to have a chat with Hank. Fill him in on what we know. I'll be back the day after tomorrow."

"Sure, no problems."

"And keep an eye on Kane. I know he's pissed about this. We all are, but I don't want him doing something stupid. Again."

"I'll keep an eye on him."

"Thank you."

———

BLACK SHIELD INDUSTRIES, WASHINGTON, D.C.

A cell phone rang on the hardwood desk of a large office and was picked up by a man wearing an Armani suit.

"Yes?"

"It's done."

"Are they going to be a problem?"

"Maybe."

"We'll have to keep an eye on them. If there's a problem, we'll have to take care of it."

"Exactly."

———

PENTAGON, WASHINGTON, D.C.— THE NEXT DAY

"You were told to leave this alone, Mary," General Hank Jones, chairman of the Joint Chiefs growled in his deep voice.

Thurston stared at Jones. He was a big man in his late sixties. He reminded her of the former general, Norman Schwarzkopf. His office was a traditional wood-paneled affair with a small American flag on a staff in the right rear corner next to a large window.

"What I'm telling you is what my people found out before Horn and his team came banging on our door."

Jones raised his eyebrows. "Horn was there?"

"Yes, sir."

"Then this *is* serious."

"Yes, sir. I'm just worried that Kane might have pushed him too far. Do you know who the order came from about us handing over what we had?"

"It came from the vice-president."

"Do you think he's involved?"

"I don't know. I'll look into it on the quiet."

"Be careful, General. I don't like this at all."

CHAPTER 3

THE SUNSHINE CLUB, LOS ANGELES, CALIFORNIA

THE BASS BEAT seemed to pound through the skulls of the dancers; it was so loud. More than half of them were in a drug-induced fugue as they jumped up and down with the music. The heat in the room was almost unbearable, resulting in the majority of dancers, men and women, discarding their outer garments.

Sweat-lathered bodies glistened under the strobe lights while the DJ turned the volume up another notch.

Remy Burton breasted the bar and took a bottle of water offered to her by the young man on the other side. He leaned forward and shouted to be heard, "Looking good tonight, Remy!"

She looked down impulsively at her sweat-sheened body. She was lithe, toned, her stomach muscles well-defined. Her round breasts were held up by a white bikini top while her lower parts were covered by tight, denim cutoffs.

Remy was in her mid-twenties, her long dark hair tied

back in a ponytail that hung down her back. She smiled at the guy behind the bar and leaned across and grasped his T-shirt. She pulled him close and kissed him on the lips. His parted and her tongue darted fleetingly inside his mouth. He drew back and said, "Hey, I'm working here."

She smiled seductively and said, "I'll see you when you're finished, Tom?"

"You bet. You want something other than water?"

"Sure. Give me a beer."

Tom came back with her beer and took the money she offered. Remy took a sip and placed it back on the bar.

"Hey, bitch, we've been looking for you everywhere!"

Remy turned to see Lara and Beth smiling at her. "Where have you been?" Remy shouted above the noise of the quickened bass.

"What?" Lara yelled.

"I said, where have you been?"

They shook their heads and signaled her to follow them. Remy started to but remembered her beer. She turned back and scooped it off the bar, then followed her friends. They found a table surrounded by low chairs in a secluded corner and sat down. With two hefty swigs, Remy rid herself of the beer.

They sat and talked, or rather yelled at each other for the next five or so minutes. They were soon approached by a young man dressed in white pants and a white singlet top. He sat down and shouted, "Hello!"

The three girls stared at him and giggled.

"What is so funny?" he asked with the hint of an accent.

Remy leaned forward. "You look like Don Johnson."

Remy's friends giggled some more because he actually did look like the eighties' television star.

"Who is Don Johnson?" he asked.

"Miami Vice?"

The young man gave her a blank expression.

Remy took out her I-Phone and tapped the screen. After a couple of moments, she turned it around and showed him who Don Johnson was.

"That is Don Johnson?"

"Yes."

"I must be very good looking then."

This brought forth more chuckles.

"Let me buy you all a drink," he said.

Remy shook her head. "No, thanks."

"Come on, Remy. Another one won't hurt," Lara urged her. Then she looked at the young man and asked, "What's your name?"

"Dominik."

"We'll all have a drink, Dominik," Lara said. "It can't hurt."

———

Remy didn't notice the increased temperature at first. She just thought it was the heat from the crush of bodies on the dance floor. But when she sat down, it didn't stop. In fact, her temperature seemed to increase. She swallowed a bottle of water in two gulps. However, it wasn't enough, and she wanted more.

"Are you OK?" Beth asked her friend.

"I don't know. I'm so hot. I want some more water."

"I'll get it," Dominik told her.

"It's OK. I'll..." Remy tried to stand but felt faint and sat back down.

"Stay here," Dominik told her.

Remy started to shake. Not much at first, then it grew in intensity until she was having a full-blown seizure.

"Remy!" Beth screamed. "Remy!"

Her eyes rolled back into her head, leaving only the whites visible and she lost consciousness. Lara jumped to her feet and screamed, "Help us! Somebody, help us!"

The music was too loud. Nobody came. Not even Dominik.

Ten minutes later, Remy Burton was dead.

TEAM REAPER HQ, EL PASO, TEXAS

Thurston replaced the phone handset as though it were made of fragile glass and let her hand linger on it while she processed what she'd just been told. Dread filled her heart at the thought of what she had to do. But before she did, she picked the phone up and punched in a memorized number.

The general waited and then said, "Come into my office for a moment."

A few minutes later the door opened, and Kane walked in.

"Close the door," she said to him.

He did so and stood at ease in front of her desk. "What's up?"

"I just got off the phone to a detective in the LAPD. Did you know Axe had a sister?"

"Sure. He never talks about her though. Keeps his family stuff to himself. His parents are dead. Been so for a while now." Kane frowned. "Has something happened to her?"

Thurston nodded. "She was DOA at UCLA Medical Center last night."

The shock registered on Kane's face. "Christ, what happened?"

"Bad reaction to MDMA."

"Drugs? Really?"

"That's what the detective said."

"Axe is going to crack. He despises drugs and to hear that his sister died of an overdose, that's going to near enough kill him."

"I was hoping you'd be there when I tell him. You being his friend."

Kane nodded. "I can tell him if you like. Might be better coming from me."

Thurston shook her head. "No. I'm his commander. I'll do it."

They left the office and found Axe in the team's makeshift gym. He was stripped down to his shorts, lifting weights. His muscles rippled each time he moved. Watching them enter, he said jokingly, "You all come to see how a real man does it?"

He gave them a broad smile which disappeared as soon as the grin wasn't returned. "What's up?" he asked.

Thurston's pained expression just added to his angst. "Come on, guys, it can't be that bad."

But it was.

———

UCLA MEDICAL CENTER, LOS ANGELES

The lift to the second floor seemed to take the longest time. The presence of the detective made the ride ten times worse.

Kane and Axe stood at the back of the elevator, their

mood a somber one. On the other side of Axe stood Cara. Beside the detective was Thurston.

The elevator stopped, and the doors slid open. Everyone except Axe stepped out into the sterile-smelling hall. He hesitated. Maybe he thought that if he didn't see Remy, it would be less real, not true.

"Axe," Kane said in a soft voice.

"Hmmm?"

"It's time to go, dude."

With tears in his eyes, Axe looked at his friend. "I don't know if I can, Reaper."

Kane stepped back onto the lift and pressed the button for the top floor. The others watched as the doors closed, and they disappeared.

"Where are they going?" the detective asked.

Thurston said, "Give them some time. They'll be back.

———

The lift went halfway between floors before Kane hit the stop button. Then he and Axe sat on the floor of the elevator and talked about nothing particular. Just shooting the shit. About the Corps, different ops they'd been on, friends they'd lost along the way. Eventually, the conversation came around to Remy.

"I can't believe she's gone, man," Axe said. "Not this way. Remy didn't do drugs. Sure, she liked to have a drink every now and then. Who doesn't? But not drugs. I won't believe it."

Axe talked some more about her while Kane listened. Of times when they were growing up when their parents had died. One from cancer, the other had had a stroke. It had been Remy who'd moved in with them to take care of them both. Axe had been on deployment. Hell, he was always on deployment back then.

The big man went silent, and Kane said, "You ready, buddy?"

He nodded. "Yeah."

Kane started the elevator again, and they went back to the second floor. When they stepped off, they found the others still there waiting for them. "We all good?" Thurston asked.

Kane nodded.

Cara looped her arm through Axe's and held him close as they took the journey toward the morgue together. Once there, the attendant already had Remy laid out for identification. Axe had seen dead people before, some in the most horrible, disfigured ways possible, but none of them had been his sister.

When Remy was covered back up, Axe's gaze settled on the detective. "What are you doing about this?"

The detective, whose name was Rogers said, "What do you mean?"

"My sister didn't do drugs."

"That's what her friends said," he allowed.

"So, how did it get into her system?"

"We think her drink was spiked."

"By who?"

"We're not sure. We think it was by a young man she met at The Sunshine Club."

"You think?"

Rogers moved uncomfortably. "We haven't been able to locate him for questioning."

"Oh, for fuck's sake," Axe hissed. He turned to Thurston. "Ma'am, request permission for leave?"

"If it's for what I think it's for, Axel, then no."

Axe wasn't about to let it go. "This is what we do,

ma'am. We find the bad guys with the drugs and put them down."

"No."

"I just want to talk to her friends is all."

"I can go with him, ma'am," Kane put in.

"Me too," said Cara.

"We'll all go," Thurston stated after giving it some thought.

"I hope you all aren't about to interfere in an ongoing police investigation?" Rogers protested.

Thurston took out her identification and showed him. "See this? It's what gives me the authority to do just that."

"What the hell is The Worldwide Drug Initiative?"

"That's us," Thurston informed him.

"And what is it you do exactly?"

Cara stared at him without blinking. "We kill bad guys."

––––––

CULVER CITY

Lara and Beth lived on the bottom floor of a three-story brick apartment block in Culver City. It was after dark when the four team members arrived and knocked on the door. Lara was the one who opened it, and her shock was evident when she saw Axe and the others standing before her.

"Axel...I...I'm so, so sorry," she said and then fell apart.

The big man took her slight frame in his arms and held her. In the entryway, Beth appeared. "Axel? Is that you?"

Then he was holding two young women in his bear of an embrace.

After a minute or so, he said in a soft voice, "Can we come in please, girls?"

They stepped back, wiped at their eyes, and then nodded, admitting the team to their small but comfortable apartment.

Axe introduced everybody once they were inside. After that was done, he said, "We need to know about what happened."

"Are you going to try and figure out why Remy is dead?"

Nodding, Axe said, "Maybe."

"She never took drugs, Axel," Lara said adamantly. "There's no way in hell she'd knowingly do so. It's my fault."

"Whoa," said Axe. "Where's this coming from?"

"A guy offered to buy us all drinks. Remy didn't want one. I told her it couldn't...hurt."

"That's not your fault," Cara said. "You weren't to know her drink was going to get spiked. It could have been any one of you."

"She's right," Thurston added. "The only one to blame in all of this is the one who did it."

Lara lost it again, and Thurston moved in beside her as a mother would try to comfort her daughter.

"Who was the guy that bought the drinks?" Axe asked Beth.

"He said his name was Dominik."

"Have you ever seen him before?" Kane asked.

Beth shook her head. "No. I don't even think he was American?"

Kane glanced at Cara. The latter asked, "Why do you think that?"

"He had no idea who Don Johnson was or Miami Vice when we joked about what he was wearing."

"Do they have CCTV at the club you were at?"

"I think so. Tom would know."

"Who's Tom?" Axe asked.

Lara looked up at him. "He's Remy's part-time boyfriend."

The big man was confused. "Part-time? I didn't know she was seeing anyone."

"It was an on again, off again type of relationship. But lately, it was more on than off."

A picture on the far wall caught Axe's eye. He walked across to it and stared. The photo showed Lara, Beth, and Remy, arms across each other's shoulders. The three amigos. She...they all looked so happy.

"That was taken down in Baja last year," Beth told him. "We had such a great time."

He remembered the first time he'd taken Remy down there after both of their parents were gone. It was like a giant release for his sister and because he'd been away so much, a getting to know you again trip for Axe.

Truth be told, it was the greatest week of his life. He'd learned so much about her, and now she was gone. It wasn't fair. He turned to face Beth. "Can you do me a favor?"

"Sure."

"Can you and Lara pack up all of Remy's stuff for me?"

"Don't you want to do it? What about stuff that you want to keep?"

"Just box it up, and I can look through it later."

"OK. But what about her service. When will that be?"

Oh shit! He had no idea. "I'll let you know." His gaze turned to Thurston who saw the look of utter fear etched on his face. It was all starting to sink in. He could fight men who wanted to kill him in hand-to-hand combat and not flinch. But he had no idea how to deal with this. The general gave him a knowing nod.

Axe cleared his throat. "Can I use your bathroom?"

"Sure, it's through there," Beth told him.

Axe disappeared, and Kane caught Thurston's eye. She nodded, and he and Cara walked toward the front door.

———

"Where you going, buddy?" Kane asked a startled Axe as he appeared around the side of the building.

"Fuck, Reaper, you just about gave me a damned heart attack," Axe gasped.

"You didn't answer the question. Where?"

A car flashed past under the orange lights on the street. The night was cool, yet Axe was sweating. He was angry and needed someone to blame for the death of his sister. The only way to do that was to find the young man named Dominik. He said, "I'm going to the club."

Kane shook his head. "Bad idea. The general only agreed to come and talk to the girls. Not to go off chasing after our tails."

"I don't care. I need to find this fucker who's responsible for Remy's death."

"You can't do it this way, Axe," Cara said to him. "Not running off on your own."

"I can take care of myself."

"But that's not what the team is about," said Thurston, adding her voice to the conversation. "So, you either do like I say, or you're out."

Anger flashed through Axe at the ultimatum. "Then what do you suggest...ma'am?"

"You, Kane, and Cara go to the club and see if you can look at the CCTV. I'm going to get things moving with your sister's service."

Axe's jaw dropped. "Ma'am..."

"It's fine. I can do it. I really don't mind, but I may need you to answer any questions which arise."

"Yes, ma'am. Thank you, ma'am."

"Good. Go and see what you can find out."

————

THE SUNSHINE CLUB

When they walked inside the club, Kane was well conscious of the M17 tucked into the back of his jeans. Before the security guard at the front door could check him, Kane flashed the Worldwide Drug Initiative identification in front of his face.

"We're here to see Tom," he'd told him.

"What about?"

"That's our business."

The big man had stepped aside, and the three of them entered. Loud music assailed their ears, and the normal crush of dancers on the floor was non-existent. The track that was playing finished and it was followed by the booming of the DJ's voice which seemed overly extreme considering the current state of the room.

Even though the crowd was thin, a stale sweat stench still hung heavily in the air.

"It's kind of quiet in here," Cara said, wrinkling her nose. "Not like I expected."

They reached the bar, and a girl in a singlet top and jeans approached them. "Can I help you?"

"We're looking for Tom," Kane told her.

"Who are you?"

Kane showed his credentials. She nodded and said, "I'll get him."

A few minutes later Tom appeared. He took one look at Axe and said, "You're him. Remy's brother?"

Axe nodded. "I am."

"I only saw pictures of you."

"I knew nothing of you."

"What do you want to know?"

"We want to see CCTV footage of the night Remy died," Kane said.

"I'm not sure I can..."

Kane showed him his credentials and said, "Now."

Tom took them out back to a small office where everything was set up. Cara said, "Quiet night out there?"

"Someone dying in a club will do that," he said bluntly.

Tom found the CCTV footage, and they watched it in silence. They saw Dominik come into shot near the bar and then keep walking toward the door. "That's the guy who bought the drinks, there."

They then saw people start to move toward where Remy and the others were. Tom paused it. "You don't want to watch it from here."

Kane said, "Rewind it."

Tom did and then hit play. They got to the bit where Dominik bought the drinks. He'd been served by Tom. The four of them watched it further and saw him pick up the tray and walk away from the bar. Cara frowned. "I didn't see him put anything in any of the drinks. He blocked the view of the camera."

"Is there another angle?" Kane asked.

Tom hit keys on the keyboard, and the view changed. They could see him more clearly now. They watched on, the beers arrived, and Dominik went to pick up the tray. As he did so, he waved his hand over the top of it and then grabbed it with both hands.

"He's good," Kane said. "I'd say he's done this more than once."

"Fucking asshole," Axe rumbled.

They watched on further to where he arrived at the table again. He held out the tray and let the girls take their own drinks. "Son of a bitch," Cara said in disbelief. "Remy wasn't his target. They all were. It was like Russian roulette. Remy just happened to be the unlucky one who grabbed the wrong beer."

"But why?" Tom asked.

"MDMA can be used as a date-rape drug. Unlike Rohypnol, MDMA stimulates the victim and overcomes all the inhibitions that they would normally have. Unfortunately, it looks like Remy chose the wrong drink and had a bad reaction to it."

Kane said, "Bring up the camera at the door. I want to see if he came in alone."

Tom's fingers punched at the keys again, and a vision of the outside came up in a panoramic view. People came and went in a constant stream, all checked by security. Then Dominik appeared, flanked by two men. They walked past the line and up to the security guard. Had a discussion and the big guy stepped aside to let them in.

Just as they were about to enter, three more men appeared. Nothing like the others. These guys had gang literally tattooed all over them.

"Who are they?" Axe asked.

Tom frowned. "Gangbangers. Hang on." He worked

the keyboard, and the picture zoomed in. He focused on the tattoos and drew in a sharp breath. "They're *El Diablos*."

"Who the fuck are they?" Axe snapped.

"They're bad. They're really bad. They do everything from drug trafficking to extortion and murder."

They watched on as words were traded between the two groups and then Dominik walked away from the head of the line with them. The security guard watched them go. One of the gangbangers noticed his gaze and said something to him. The security guard turned away.

In the background, Kane saw things exchanged. Even though the picture was grainy, it wasn't hard to tell that it was a drug deal. Once done, they all shook hands and went their separate ways.

"They seem awfully friendly," Cara said. "Especially if these guys are meant to be so tough and all."

"They are, believe me," Tom assured them.

"So that's where the son of a bitch got the Ecstasy from," Axe growled.

"It still doesn't tell us who he is," Kane said. "Can you give us a copy of that please, Tom?"

Tom nodded.

Reaper turned to the others. "If we give this to Slick, he might be able to come up with something."

"What about that *El Diablo* fucker?" Axe asked.

"Slick should be able to get us a name."

"Why don't we just go and rattle his fucking cage?" Axe growled.

Tom snorted with sarcasm, drawing the built-up wrath of Axe. He took a couple of steps toward the barman and began to drag him from his chair. "You got something to say, motherfucker? Huh? Come on, spill. Then I'll ram your teeth down your fucking throat."

Kane grabbed his friend and pulled him away. "Easy, big feller. You weren't the only one who lost something here. He did too, remember? Just cool it."

Axe whirled and hissed, "*Fuck you!* She was my sister. She was all the family I had left."

Reaper grabbed him by the shoulders. "We're your family too, Axe. You've still got us, buddy."

"Shit," Axe said and looked at Tom. "Sorry, man."

For the first time, Tom's face showed some emotion, but it quickly disappeared when he said, "You can't just go in and confront these guys. It's like signing your own death warrant."

Kane nodded. "First we'll see what Slick has to say. Then we'll go rattle his cage."

CHAPTER 4

WEST COAST MOTEL, EAST LOS ANGELES

ACCORDING TO SLICK, the *El Diablos* were a clique of the 18th Street Gang. A more brutal, bloody, violent clique of an already brutal gang. The 18th Street gang started near 18th Street and Union Avenue in the Rampart District of Los Angeles. Originally, they had been part of the Clanton 14 gang. Some of the gang members wanted to form a new part of the gang called Clanton 18 and allow immigrants to join. But the idea was rejected, so they split anyway and became the 18th Street Gang. Thus, condemning both gangs to a bitter rivalry.

It was said that the 18th Street Gang had up to sixty thousand members across the US. The *El Diablos* were killers. To get in, there was only one way. You had to kill a member of a rival gang. To get out, you had to be dead. There was no other way.

"You'd do well to stay away from these guys, Reaper," he said.

Thurston could see in his eyes that the warning had fallen on deaf ears. Instead, Kane said, "Tell me about the guys in the picture."

A small pointer fell on the picture on the laptop screen. Swift said, "I have no idea who the young Don Johnson here is. I've tried, but I can't get a fix on him anywhere. I even tried the name Dominik and came up empty. My guess is he lied about his name."

"Christ," Kane heard Thurston swear. He looked at Axe whose face remained passive.

"What about the gangbangers?"

"I told you to leave it be, Reaper. They're bad."

"Spill, Slick."

A picture of a young Hispanic man came up on the computer screen. He was armed with two MAC-11s and had tattoos on his arms. His smile was highlighted by a gold tooth. Swift's voice said, "This is *El Martillo*. The Hammer. He's the *El Diablos'* shot-caller."

"Their what?" Axe asked.

"Shot-caller. Their boss. That's what they call them."

"Uh huh. Where do we find him?" asked Axe.

"They have a house in a South L.A. neighborhood. Cops stay away from it unless they have to go in there. And even then, they take S.W.A.T. with them."

"Can you get us an address?" Kane asked.

"You can't seriously be considering going in there?" Swift said.

Kane said, "Not considering, going. Get us that address."

Thurston said, "I'll make a call and see if I can get you all some gear. Something more than your M17s."

"Much appreciated, ma'am."

"Get some rest. You'll go tonight. Once Slick gets us an address, I'll see if we can pull an aerial view of it. Just understand this," her expression grew grim. "Once you go in there, you're on your own. There's no air support, no QRF, nothing. Unless I can find some comms gear, you won't even have that. Copy?"

"Yes, ma'am."

Cara said, "General, could you see if you can get me some kind of weapon I can use for overwatch? I'm going to be more useful that way. If things go south, I can send a few lightning bolts their way."

"I'll see what I can do, though I can't promise anything. Now, get the hell out of here so I can make some calls."

They all went back to their rooms. Kane was only in his for five minutes when there was a soft knock at the door. He opened it, and Cara was standing there. She said, "You got a minute?"

"Sure, come on in."

She entered and instantly screwed up her nose. "Yours smells just as bad as mine."

Kane chuckled. "Like someone shit in here?"

"Yeah. Like that."

She sat on his bed and crossed her legs. There was a look of concern on her face. Kane asked, "What is it?"

"I'm worried about Axe," she said.

"Why?"

"Come on, Reaper. You know why. He's just lost his sister, and now we're going into a damned hot zone where we'll all need clear heads."

"He'll be fine," Kane said dismissively.

Cara didn't like it. "Don't do that, Reaper. 'He'll be fine' won't fucking cut it."

"What do you want me to do, Cara? Bench him?"

She shook her head. "No. But you need to find out

where his head is at. Talk to him. And if he's not squared away, then bench him."

Kane nodded. "All right. I'll talk to him."

"And if he ain't right?"

"I'll bench him."

Cara nodded. "Good enough."

"Anything else?"

"Nope. That's about it."

"Then, as the boss said, get some rest."

Cara paused.

"There is something else, isn't there?"

Cara sighed. She studied his face which still bore signs of their previous mission. "Do you want to talk about the last op? You've not said anything about it since we finished."

"No. Nothing to say."

She looked at him skeptically. "They just about killed you, Reaper. The CIA burned you. Aren't you just a little bit pissed?"

"Nothing I can do about it. Just concentrate on the here and now."

Nodding, Cara said, "All right then. I'll see you after."

She started toward the door.

"Cara?"

She turned. "Yes?"

"Thanks for caring."

"Someone has to or all you big macho shitheads would have endless psychological issues." She smiled. "Oops! Too late."

"Get out of here."

Late that afternoon when they all met in Thurston's room, all the equipment she could gather was there waiting on her bed. Off the top were two MP5SDs complete with their integrated silencers.

The MP5s came with four spare fully-loaded, thirty-round magazines, and the fire selector on the side of them could be set to either safe, semi-automatic, burst, or full auto. They also had the reputation of being one of the most accurate weapons of their type.

Cara's wish had been answered too. Beside the MP5s was a new M110A1 as it was known in the U.S. military. The weapon itself had started to be rolled out after testing in 2017. It was made by Heckler and Koch as a variant of the G28 and HK417 combined. It was the nominated replacement for the M110 SASS and came with a mounted scope, bipod, and a suppressor. Well, as suppressed as it could be.

Beside it lay two twenty-round box magazines, fully-loaded. The A1 only had two firing modes; safe and semi-auto. Forty rounds were all that Cara would require.

Further along the bed were three tactical vests and comm sets. Kane nodded. "The boss has done well."

"It's all I could manage on short notice," Thurston said by way of apology.

Cara picked up the A1. "This is sweet, ma'am. I like this. Any chance...?"

"It's going back when we've finished," Thurston said. "There's no NVGs."

"I think we'll manage," Kane said. "Axe?"

"Yeah. We'll kick some ass with these."

Thurston's expression hardened. Her gaze focused on the big ex-recon marine. "You're not there to kick ass, Axe. You're there to get answers. If I have any inkling to the contrary, I'll bench you and go myself. Do you understand?"

"Yes, ma'am."

She sighed and directed them to the small table. On it was a picture of the area where they would be inserting. One of the buildings had a circle around it. "OK. This is where our boy hides out. An old furniture factory. This whole block is slated for redevelopment. Except once the *El Diablos* moved in, all progress went on hold."

Kane studied the picture in silence for two full minutes. Beside him, Cara did the same. After he was done, he glanced up at her. "What do you think?"

She stabbed a finger at the building across the street. It seemed to have a flat rooftop accessible from the street via an external stairway. "I can set up there."

He nodded and used his own finger as a pointer. "We'll leave our transport in the alley on the blindside of the building and walk in on foot. Once we reach the front, we'll have to cross the street fast. Cara, you hit the streetlights before we go."

"Copy."

"Every one of the assholes is going to be carrying," Axe said. "More than likely we'll have to put one or more of them down before we even get inside."

"If we have to," Kane agreed. "Cara, if shit goes south, you need to keep an exfil route open for us."

"All right, Reaper."

"Listen, you three," Thurston interrupted. "Just because you make it back to your vehicle doesn't mean you're home free. The *El Diablos* control a whole lot of territory around there. Say around ten blocks in either direction. And they'll be heavily armed. If you get in the shit, I can't help you. The cops won't go in there after dark."

Kane stared her in the eye. "We've got this, ma'am."

"Make sure you do."

CHAPTER 5

"REAPER ONE, COMMS CHECK. OVER."

"Copy, Reaper One," Thurston replied, hating the fact that she was more or less flying blind.

"Reaper Team about to move to the target, Bravo. Will remain on VOX. Out."

VOX was short for Voice Operated Exchange. It worked when it picked up a sound instead of the users having to push the usual transmit button. Which meant that every time one of the team spoke, Thurston would hear it. It wasn't the same as having a drone or satellite overhead, but at least she had ears on.

Kane adjusted his tactical vest and made sure his M17 was secure. He checked the magazine on the MP5 and made sure there was a 9mm round in the breach. He turned and saw Cara slapping home the box magazine on the A1 and closing the ejector which in turn loaded a 7.62 bullet into it ready to fire.

The alley where they were parked was dark, whereas,

at both ends, orange street lights cast their dull glow. To get the SUV to where it was stopped, they had to weave through mounds of rubbish. As they'd driven along it, a dog had bolted in front of the vehicle, disturbed from where it had its nose buried in a rotting pile. The main problem was, the end of the alley towards which the SUV was pointing was blocked by a wrecked car, which meant they would have to reverse out. Quite a feat if they were under fire.

"You ready?" Kane asked them.

"Yes," Cara answered.

"Axe?"

"Yeah."

"All right. Bravo. Reaper Team moving."

"Copy, Reaper One."

Kane brought the MP5 up and started along the alley toward the wrecked car. Cara behind him, while Axe brought up the rear. When they reached the vehicle, they could see that it had once been a Chevy. Now, however, all its windows were gone, the wheels too, every panel was dented, and the interior had been carved up and stripped.

Reaper eased a glance around the corner and found the street empty. He moved as far as the stairs and waited for Cara. "This is your stop," he said.

"Uh huh," she grunted and started up the narrow metal rungs.

Once Cara had reached the top, she made her way to the front of the roof. Crouching down, she dropped the legs of the bipod, resting it on the ledge, and did a quick sweep of the immediate area.

"Looks like they've got themselves a bit of a rave going on, Reaper," Cara said into her mike. "I've got loud music, and five tangos out front. Three looked to be armed with Mac Elevens."

"Copy, Reaper Two," Kane acknowledged. "One of them wouldn't be our Hammer, would it?"

"Negative."

Kane sighed. Nothing could be that easy. "Copy. We're moving now."

He and Axe edged to the front corner of the building. They stopped, and Reaper studied the five people across the other side of the street. He eased himself back and said, "Reaper Two, copy?"

"Copy, Reaper One."

"Are those five the only ones there?"

"Roger."

"Bravo? You copy?"

"Copy, Reaper One."

"Request permission to use lethal force on the tangos out front of the target building."

"Negative, Reaper One. ROEs are that you only fire if fired upon."

Axe bit back a curse.

"Copy, Bravo. Sticking to ROEs."

"What now?" Axe asked.

"I guess we go and ask nicely," Kane told him. "Reaper Two, any change in personnel?"

"Negative, Reaper One."

"Copy. Reaper One and Four are moving."

Kane lowered his MP5 and held it in a non-threatening manner. Axe did the same. However, the weapons could be brought into action quickly when required. Then he stepped around the corner and started toward the old furniture factory.

———

"What the fuck?" Mateo hissed when he saw the two men approaching the small group. "Eh, Ignacio, get a look at this."

All of them, two women and three men, were dressed in jeans and singlet tops, exposing various tattoos.

The one called Ignacio turned to stare. His eyes widened in surprise. He started to bring up his MAC-11 but the two men were faster, and their MP5s were trained on them before Ignacio could get the thing aimed.

"Drop the fucking weapons!" Kane snarled. "Do it! Put them down!"

With a snarl, Ignacio kept the MAC-11 rising. Reaper squeezed the trigger on the MP5 twice. Both 9mm rounds hammered into the gangbanger's chest and put him down. To his right, another one tried to get a shot off, but a 7.62 slug whistled out of the night and hammered into his upper chest.

Axe's suppressed weapon settled on the center mass of Mateo. He shook his head. "Don't."

Mateo thought better of it and dropped the MAC-11 to the ground. Beside him, a young woman held a semi-automatic handgun waist high. Kane stared into her cold eyes and said to her in a calm voice, "I'll give you three heartbeats to drop the gun, or you'll end up like your friend."

Uncertainty etched her face as she looked down at the fallen man. She dropped the handgun at her feet. Reaper nodded. "Wise choice."

The young lady next to her stood wide-eyed, used to being on the other side of death. Glancing at Axe, Kane said, "Zip ties."

Axe passed them over. Kane said to Mateo, "Get on your knees. Turn around."

Mateo screwed his face up. "You a dead man, *puta*."

"If you don't do what he says, Pablo, you won't be around to fucking find out," Axe hissed.

They managed to get the three remaining gang members bundled up and make gags from the singlet of one of the dead men. Reaper stared into the eyes of Mateo and asked, "Where can I find The Hammer?"

Mateo spit at him.

The balled right fist traveled no more than a foot before it crashed into the gang member's face. His eyes rolled back in his head, and he slumped to his side, out cold. Kane turned his attention to the women. *"El Martillo?"*

One remained stoic, but the other's eyes gave her away. She glanced at the building. Kane said into his mic, "Reaper Two, copy?"

"Copy."

"We're going inside. You are cleared hot."

"Copy, Reaper One."

Kane stared hard at the women. "I have a friend who is going to watch over you. If you move or try to escape, she will put a bullet in your heads."

Kane and Axe moved to the door and opened it. They slipped inside and immediately were seen by one of those within.

The old factory had been cleaned out and was now just one big room with old furniture and such scattered around it. At its center stood a large drum with flames shooting from the top of it.

"Central fucking heating," Axe whispered.

The *El Diablos* were gathered in small groups. Kane estimated from one sweep of his eyes that there were maybe twenty present.

"Who the fuck are you?" a voice snarled.

Everyone inside the factory shifted their gaze to the

two men. The pumping music ceased, and weapons started to appear. Before the shit hit the fan, Kane said, "I'm here to see The Hammer."

A tattooed man stepped forward. "What you want with him, *cabrón*? Tell us quick before we kill you."

"Are you him?"

"No."

"Then, where is he?"

The man shrugged.

Axe's whisper filled Kane's ear. "Reaper, the bed."

He shifted his gaze and saw a metal-framed double bed against the far wall. It was covered with stained blankets and pillows. But there was also something else. A woman. Dirty, disheveled, face puffy and bloody from beatings she'd received. Then he saw the chains, and that changed everything.

"Bravo," he said, his voice almost inaudible. "We've got a woman chained to a bed. Looks like our friends here have been abusing her for a good while. Request permission to step it up a bit."

There was a pause from Thurston's end.

"What did you say, *hijo de puta*?"

"Boss? I need an answer."

The gangbanger took a threatening step forward.

Dead air.

"Now would be good."

Thurston's voice filled his ear. "OK, do it."

The MP5 in Reaper's hands spat once, stopping the man in his tracks. A look of disbelief appeared on his face, and he looked down at the dark stain starting to spread across his white singlet. "*Ay caramba*."

Dropping to his knees, he slumped forward. Kane raised his voice. "I'm looking for *El Martillo*."

There was movement to his right and the man they sought stepped forward. "I am *El Martillo*."

Kane nodded. "Step over here."

The man remained still, holding his ground.

"Now, motherfucker," Axe growled.

Martillo's eyes flashed his anger threatening to spill over. No one spoke to him this way. Let alone come into his territory and kill one of his own the way these two had done.

"How did you get past my men?" he asked.

"Put it this way," Kane explained, "two of them won't wake up tomorrow, one will have a headache, and the two ladies will be fine unless they do something stupid. Now get the fuck over here."

The shot-caller moved forward stiffly. He stopped just short of Kane, his jaw set firm, chin out in an act of defiance. Reaper reached into his pocket and pulled out a picture. He placed it in front of Martillo's face and asked him, "Who is this guy you're with?"

Martillo shook his head. "I've never seen him before."

"Take a good look at the dick beside him. Isn't that you? I think it might be." Kane lifted the MP5 so that the suppressor was pushed up under the shot-caller's chin. "Answer the damn question."

The shot-caller shrugged.

Kane lowered the MP5 and shot him in the leg.

The Hammer fell.

A cry of pain escaped his lips, and he lay there clutching at his shattered leg. Thurston's voice filled Kane's comms. "Reaper? What just happened?"

"Our man just fell over, Bravo. Nothing major."

The crowd started to move, and Axe snapped his MP5 into line with the nearest one. "Don't even think about it, fuck face. Not unless you want to end up worse than your friend here."

The man's top lip curled. "You are a dead man."

"Shut the hole in your face."

Kane leaned down. He showed Martillo the picture again. "Who is he?"

"His name is Bazyli," Martillo hissed. "Bazyli Marek."

"Kane, you need to get out of there. It's taking too long."

"Where is he?"

"He stays at the Sunset Plaza."

"Bravo, you get that?"

"Copy."

"How do you know him?" Kane asked.

"His father supplies us with Ecstasy."

"He's European?"

"Yes. Poland."

"Shit," Kane swore and stood up. "All right, everybody take a couple of steps back. Axe, get the girl."

Once she was free, they began backing towards the exit. "Just so you know, I have someone outside with a bigger gun than the ones we're using. If any of you poke your heads outside before we leave, she'll blow it off."

"You are fucking dead, asshole," Martillo shouted after them. "I'll kill you, your family, your family's family, even your fucking dog!"

Kane paused. If there was one thing he'd learned as a recon marine, it was never to leave a dangerous enemy on your backtrail. He raised the MP5 and shot Martillo in the head.

———

WEST COAST MOTEL, EAST LOS ANGELES

Their exfil was uneventful. The *El Diablos* were too shocked at the cold killing of their shot-caller to do anything. On the way back to the motel, they dropped the young woman off at the nearest hospital.

Now, back at the motel, they weren't even out of their tactical gear, and Thurston was tearing strips off the team leader.

"What the fuck was that?" she hissed at him.

"That was me getting the job done," Kane growled back.

"No! No, it wasn't. That was fucking tantamount to cold-blooded killing."

"Bullshit!" Kane shot back. "The killing was justified. They had a young woman there that they were raping at will. They sell drugs, and god knows what else and would have tried to kill us when we left. The prick's final mistake was threatening me."

"Still no cause for what you did," Thurston snapped.

Reaper just stared at her.

"When we get back to El Paso, you are going to see someone. Get your head straight. I think that stint under-cover with the gang fucked it up."

"I'm fine."

"You're not. This isn't a fucking democracy, Kane. I'm the boss. You do it, or you're out."

He stared at her defiantly. Then something broke through his anger which told him she was right. But instead of acknowledging it, he turned and walked away.

"Where are you going, Kane?"

As he walked out the door, he said, "Nowhere."

———

HAMP'S BAR AND GRILL, EAST LOS ANGELES

Kane took a long pull of his beer and sat it back on the bar. He'd cooled down some since leaving the motel, but there was still turmoil within the usually cool warrior's exterior.

He looked about. Even though it was early morning, the bar was still busy. Along the counter from him sat a drunk in a suit. Next to the suit was a hooker doing her best to separate the man from his money. No doubt she utilized the alley next to the bar. Many of the tables had someone seated at them. Behind the bar, three women dressed in jeans and too-small singlet tops supplied those on the other side with whatever they required.

Kane finished his beer and thought about getting another.

"Can I buy you one, Reaper?"

"Shit," Kane muttered, and he turned to face Iona. "What the fuck do you want?"

She was dressed in a pantsuit and looked immaculate. No one would have figured by the look of her that it was four in the morning. She smiled at him, and he noticed the bulge inside her coat where her personal sidearm was sequestered.

"Well?"

"I was hoping we might talk."

"Where's your boss?"

"He's around."

Kane studied her ice-blue eyes. "Not here though."

"No."

He waved at the woman behind the bar.

"Another, cowboy?"

"Make it two," he said, indicating Iona. "One for the lady."

"Sure."

Once she was gone, Kane stared at the CIA agent and asked, "What do you want...no. What the fuck is your name?"

"Do I sense a hint of hostility in your voice, Kane?"

"You burned me. What else do you expect?"

"I was hoping we could get past that. It wasn't anything personal," she explained. "And my name is Nicole."

"Really?" he asked with skepticism.

"Yes, really."

The woman returned with the beers, and Nicole tossed a fifty on the bar. "Keep the change."

After a long pull on his beer, Kane stared her hard in the eye and said, "Talk."

"I'm kind of curious why you and the others are in Los Angeles?"

Alarm bells rang as soon as she mentioned it. "You've been keeping tabs on us?"

Nicole shrugged.

"Why?"

"Just following orders. I must say, that little op you guys pulled tonight was pretty ballsy. Going after *El Martillo* like that."

"You were there?"

Nicole nodded.

Kane glanced around the bar. Although he'd not noticed before, he did now. Three of them. Spread out around the room. All male. From the looks, all ex-military. Reaper reached behind his back and took out the M17 and rested it on his lap for Nicole to see.

"Easy, Rambo. They don't do a thing without my say so."

"Enough of the bullshit, Nicole. Tell me what you want."

She sighed. "I'm just the messenger. You are to tell your boss to back away from whatever it is you think you're doing and go back to Texas."

Anger rose within Kane. He ground his teeth together and then said in a low voice, "We're looking for the asshole responsible for the death of Axe's sister."

"Yes. And you've fixed that little problem. Now go home."

"You mean The Hammer?"

"I do."

"He might have handed over the drugs, but he wasn't the one responsible. The one we're looking for put drugs in her drink."

Nicole nodded. "Let that be the end of it."

"Why? Who is Bazyli Marek?"

Recognition flared in her eyes.

"Yes," Kane said. "We know his name. Who is he?"

"Someone you need to leave alone," she said. Her voice was low with an edge. She climbed to her feet, and Kane's hand shot out and grabbed her arm.

Nicole's eyes glanced over his shoulder, and Kane turned to see her help on their feet. Each man had his hand inside his jacket, ready to take out whatever handgun was hidden there. Kane turned back to her and said, "Tell your boss to go fuck himself. And the next time he wants to deliver a message, come himself, and I'll be glad to ram it back down his throat."

"He is not someone you want to mess with, Kane. He's dangerous."

"So am I."

Nicole shook her hand free and stared at him one last

time. Then as she turned away, he heard her say, "You were warned."

He watched her leave and then finished his beer. Then, swore savagely. "Fuck!"

———

The window on the black SUV whirred down as Nicole approached. Inside the vehicle, Newcomb waited patiently. "Well?"

Nicole shrugged. "I don't know. If I had to guess, I'd say they're going to be a bigger problem than you figured."

"Did he say what he wanted the kid for?"

"You'll never believe this. The stupid little fuck spiked the drink of the other one's sister. She died, and now they're after him. They know his name, Mark."

"That is a problem," he sighed. "OK, I'll deal with it."

"How?"

"That's not your concern."

"If you go after them, Mark, be careful. You've seen first-hand how they operate."

"I won't have to go after them," he said with a smile. "They'll come to me."

———

WEST COAST MOTEL, EAST LOS ANGELES

"I can't believe that asshole is monitoring us," Thurston growled. "Hang on, yes I can. Son of a bitch."

"What do we do?" Cara asked.

"We can't stop now," Axe said. "We're almost there. We know where he is; all we have to do is sweep him up."

Kane said, "I agree with Axe. Are we going to let them scare us off? Besides, it's still illegal for them to be working on U.S. soil."

"We wait," Thurston said. "I want to see what Slick finds for us."

"By then it might be too late," Cara said. "We should at least get eyes on him somehow. Then if the opportunity arises, we can grab him. After all, it falls under our purview. There are drugs involved."

"All right," Thurston agreed. "But don't move on him until I give the word."

"Yes, ma'am."

"And be careful."

———

THE PENTAGON, WASHINGTON, D.C.

"Jones," the deep voice said as it answered the phone. His size matched his voice. Across the desk from him sat his morning appointment, Rear-Admiral Alexander Joseph who headed up NAVSPECWARCOM (United States Naval Special Warfare Command). He was in his fifties, gray hair, solid build, with a lined face and straight nose. His blue eyes almost matched the color of the sky.

"It's Thurston, General. Do you have a moment?"

"All the time in the world for you, Mary. Hang on, I'll put you on speaker. Alex Joseph is in the room with me. He's popped in for a visit."

He clicked a button and Joseph heard Thurston say, "Morning, Admiral."

"Morning, Mary. How's that band of no-goods you're in command of?"

"It's kind of interesting right about now, sir."

Jones frowned. "What's up, Mary?"

"The same problem as before, sir."

Jones nodded. "Speak plain, Mary. I'd say Joe has had some experience with our friend."

"Newcomb has got us under surveillance, sir. Kane ran into one of his agents this morning, the one who burned him in fact, and she tried to warn us off."

Jones looked at Joseph. The Admiral asked, "Are we talking about CIA Newcomb?"

"Yes, sir."

"He's a bad one, Mary. A dangerous man. What seems to be the issue?"

Mary filled them in on what had happened. From the death of Axe's sister, right up until Kane briefed her on the bar.

"Goddamn son of a bitch," Jones blew. "Who the fuck does he think he is?"

"What do you plan to do, Mary?" Joseph asked.

"I'd like to pick the POI up," she explained. "General, have you looked into anything?"

"There's nothing to report, yet, Mary. But, by all means, this falls under your brief as far as I'm concerned. Pick that little bastard up."

"Thank you, sir."

"Do you need any help, Mary?" Joseph asked.

"I think we'll be right, sir. Thanks."

"Before you go, Mary," Jones said. "You made the right call with Kane. Get him checked out. I don't want him getting all screwed up if it can be helped."

"What about the shooting, sir? I'm still in two minds about what to do."

"Let it go. But make sure he understands that if it happens again, then I'll bring the hammer down on him myself. Sorry about the pun."

"Thank you, sir."

CHAPTER 6

SUNSET PLAZA HOTEL, LOS ANGELES

THE BLACK SUV rolled to a stop across the street from the hotel's main entrance. Kane engaged the button to operate his electric window and peered out. It looked busy. There was an undercover parking area where guests could drive up and pass their vehicle over to a waiting valet. A small, immaculately-kept garden full of blooms stood on either side of the sliding glass entrance doors. The center portion of the hotel's front was all glass, from the ground floor up to the tenth. A restaurant on the first floor had a large outdoor dining area which overlooked the street.

Thurston said, "Are you all clear? You get the package, and I'll meet you in the alley out the back. If it is too hot, then we all walk away. The last thing we need is a firefight in a hotel full of guests."

"What about the bodyguards?" Cara asked. "They're just not going to give him up."

"As long as you don't kill them, I don't care. Now, remember, room nine-oh-six."

"All right, let's go," Kane said, opening his door.

The others followed him across the street while Thurston eased the SUV away from the curb behind them. They walked through the entrance lobby and toward the elevators. The floors were cover with white marble tiles, brass and gold fittings seemed to be everywhere they looked. Indoor plants made up a sizable garden around a water feature far off to their right.

Kane glanced over at the long counter to see if they were being observed. The staff were too busy with customers to worry about them.

They all had concealed comms, and Kane's came to life just before they reached the elevators. "Reaper, I saw at least two males back there who look like trouble."

Kane pressed the call button on the wall to go up and casually turned away. "Where, Cara?"

"Far wall near the window and another is standing near the third marble pillar."

He let his gaze drift across and then turned back toward the elevator. He said, "I've got them. Bravo? Reaper One. Copy?"

"Copy."

"Unless I miss my guess, Bravo, I'd say our friends the spooks are here. Over."

"How many?"

"Two that we can see. But I figure there's more somewhere."

There was a moment of silence before Thurston said, "It's your call, Reaper One. Walk away or continue on mission."

The elevator dinged and the doors slid open. Kane

hesitated a moment and then said, "Reaper elements continuing on mission. Out."

They stepped into the elevator, and Kane picked their floor. The doors slid shut, and Kane immediately reached around behind his back and took out his M17. The others followed his lead.

"You reckon we're going to need these?" Axe asked.

"I guess we're about to find out."

When the elevator stopped, and the doors slid open, Kane stepped out.

Nothing happened. The hallway was clear. At the rear, Kane sensed Cara and Axe fall in behind. He started along the thoroughfare's patterned blue carpet, M17 down at his side, ticking off the numbers as he went. He hugged the left side wall as he walked, Cara the right. Stepping around an artificial potted plant, Kane stopped near a door and frowned.

"What's up?" Cara asked, seeing he was troubled.

"Something's not right. Nearly every door we've passed has had no sound behind it."

"So. It's a hotel, not a club."

Shaking his head, Kane brought the M17 up and kept walking. "Like I said, something's not right."

Suddenly, his comms came to life with Thurston's urgent voice. "Reaper One, stand down. I say again, stand down and get out, now."

———

THE ALLEY

The cell rang, and Thurston picked it up. She pressed the answer key and said, "Thurston."

"Mary? Luis. You need to put a hold on your operation right away."

"Why, what's wrong?"

"Slick was able to nail your target down. His father is Gustaw Marek. He's a Polish minister in their current government. He's in charge of the Ministry of National Defence."

"Christ!" Thurston exclaimed. "They're not CIA; they're Black Shield."

"What?" Ferrero asked.

Thurston had already hung up. "Reaper One, stand down. I say again, stand down and get out, now."

Thurston looked up, and in her rearview mirror, she saw the black SUV draw slowly to a halt.

SUNSET PLAZA HOTEL

"Repeat, Bravo," Kane said.

"Kane, those men in the lobby are Black Shield. It's all fucked up. Get out of there. They anticipated that you'd come for the kid. I'll tell you the rest later. Move!"

A door toward the end of the hallway opened, and a man dressed in jeans and jacket appeared. Slung over his right shoulder was what Kane assumed to be an MP7. He took one look at the three of them and began to bring it up into a firing position.

Kane, however, was quicker. The M17 snapped into line, and he squeezed the trigger. BLAM! BLAM! The Black Shield operator took two rounds to the chest and was slammed back, falling to the floor.

Reaper opened his mouth and said in a loud, clear voice. "Contact front!" and then all hell broke loose.

"Shit!" Axe cursed and turned to meet the threat. In front of him, Cara already had her M17 up and in a firing position covering empty space.

"Back up!" Reaper snapped. "Axe, take us out. Use the stairs."

"Copy."

"Reaper, look out," Cara shouted.

Kane saw another man armed with an MP7 emerge from the room ahead. He stepped over his fallen comrade and opened fire. Bullets filled the hallway. They punched into the drywall, sending out chunks and puffs of plaster. Cara fired two shots at the shooter and saw one of them strike him in the left shoulder.

The Black Shield contractor shouted in pain and was half turned around by the force of the bullet. His finger tightened on the trigger of his weapon, and the MP7, being on full auto, stitched a line of slugs into the wall as it burned through the magazine.

"Backup!" Cara snapped.

Behind them, the elevator dinged. The doors slid back, revealing the two operators from the lobby, both with handguns drawn. Axe was right there when it transpired and turned. His hesitation was understandable. In a situation like this, it would be easy to shoot a civilian no matter how highly-trained they were. It took a fraction of a heartbeat for him to realize who they were, and he shot the first man in the head. Blood and brains sprayed across the operator's friend, painting one side of his face red. The second man snapped off a shot at Axe, but the spray of gore had made him flinch at the last moment, and the slug flew wide, burning a hole in the wall behind the big ex-marine.

Axe blew two holes in his chest and the man, a redhead, dropped like a stone.

Whirling away from the fallen, Axe hurried to the door which led through to the stairwell. He opened it and walked to the top of the stairs. Leaning over the edge, he listened intently. There were more Black Shield shooters coming up toward them. He backed away and opened the door, just about crashing into Kane and Cara.

"We ain't going that way. The fuckers are coming up."

Kane glanced at the elevator, the doors blocked open by the body of one of the operators laying half in and out of it. "Looks like that's it."

"It's a fucking death trap."

A burst of gunfire ripped along the hallway from a third shooter who emerged from the room at the end of it. Kane snapped, "Got another idea?"

"Nope."

He leaned around the corner of the alcove and fired three shots, forcing the Black Shield man back. "Go!" he snapped, and Cara and Axe moved across to the elevator.

Axe leaned down and rolled the body while Cara covered both him and Kane as he crossed over. She saw the shooter start to ease around the door jamb ahead and fired twice. Debris flew from the bullet strikes, and the man jerked back.

Cara ducked back into the elevator, and Kane pressed the button. The doors closed, shutting them into what Axe had called a death trap.

———

THE ALLEY

Thurston watched as the two men dressed in civvies climbed from the SUV and looked around casually. She noticed the bulges under their coats where their weapons were hidden.

Both men were well over six-feet tall. She guessed by their buzzcuts that both had been military at some stage. The driver was a black man, solid. His companion was also solid; though he was Caucasian with brown hair. It was him that pointed out the vehicle in which Thurston was seated.

When she had been a ranger, Mary Thurston had been on many ops, some of them behind enemy lines, others had required a certain finesse. This situation would require something else. For these men were here to kill her or her people. And she sure as shit wasn't about to let that happen.

She placed the M17 on her lap, ready to fire, right hand still holding it. Her eyes darted to the mirrors, watching their approach.

Thurston's left hand went to the door release, and she waited. Waited...

Waited...

Waited...

And then she moved.

The door flew open, and Thurston came fluidly through the opening. The Black Shield men, surprised by her sudden movements, hesitated, giving the general all the time she needed to take down the first of them with one shot to the chest.

Not waiting to see the result, Thurston shifted aim and shot the second man who almost had his weapon drawn. He dropped to the ground and his back arched. Thurston hurried up to the fallen men and shot them again. Then she glanced around, looking for any further threats.

Leaning down, she went through their pockets and

found a cell on the second man. She stuffed it in her pocket for later.

The general straightened and began walking toward their vehicle. As she did, she said, "Reaper One, copy?"

Nothing.

Thurston opened the door of the Black Shield SUV and climbed in, starting to search it.

"Reaper One, copy?"

Nothing.

———

SUNSET PLAZA HOTEL

The elevator door opened on seven, and there stood three people waiting to get on. They took one look at the SIG M17 in Kane's hand and backed away. He immediately raised his left hand and said, "It's OK. We work for the government. Go back to your room and stay there."

Not needing to be told twice, they took off like their asses were on fire and disappeared into a room.

Behind them, Kane, Cara, and Axe worked their way along the hallway toward the stairs. Cara said, "We have to get off this floor."

"Yes," Kane agreed. "The last thing we need is a firefight with civilians in the mix."

"What the hell are these Black Shield fuckers up to anyway?" Axe growled. "Why are they trying to kill us?"

"I don't know," Kane said. "But you can bet your ass that Newcomb is mixed up in this somewhere."

"*Reaper One, copy?*"

"Copy, Bravo."

"Where are you?"

"We're on seven and working our way down. We had a little trouble with assholes trying to kill us."

"Same here. I'm taking the SUV around the front. Come out that way. The back is compromised."

"The whole op is compromised," Kane muttered.

They reached the stairs and started to work their way down, Axe in the lead. On making the fifth floor, the sudden clatter of boots on the stairs reached their ears. "Pricks are coming up this way," Axe said in a low voice.

"Back up," Kane urged.

That was when the inevitable happened. Voices echoed from above as more Black Shield operators descended the steps.

Cara opened the door to five. "I guess this is it."

Kane nodded. "Yeah. Move it."

Axe closed the door behind them, and they hurried along the carpeted hallway. At the other end, a door crashed open. It was the second stairwell. Three men spilled out armed with MP7s. The leader brought his up and let loose a sustained burst of fire which turned the hallway into a deadly shooting gallery. Kane lurched to his right and crashed against a door while Cara went down on one knee and blew off the rest of her magazine, all ten rounds. The shooter jerked under the impact of at least four strikes.

"In here!" Kane shouted.

Axe and Cara dove through the opening while Kane fired his M17 at the men along the hallway. He drew back and closed the door, locking it.

"Like rats in a trap," Axe said.

Luckily the room hadn't been lit and was empty. Cara turned the sofa, so it faced the door and then crouched behind it. Axe stood there, waiting while Kane drew back the curtains from a large sliding glass door which led onto the balcony. He opened it and stepped out. Looking down, he then turned back and walked into the room.

Suddenly the door erupted in a mass of razor-sharp wooden splinters as bullets burst through it. The Black Shield operators on the other side had opened fire with their MP7s. Kane and Axe joined Cara behind the sofa. She rose and fired three shots from the fresh magazine through the shattered door before she dropped back down. Axe and Kane followed suit.

"What the fuck are we going to do now, Reaper?" Axe growled while he dropped the empty magazine from his M17 and rammed a fresh one home.

Kane pointed at the open door to the balcony. "We go that way."

Cara gave him a curious look.

Axe said, "I hate to tell you this, but I can't fucking fly."

"You don't have to," Kane told them.

Another burst of automatic fire tore through the door. A vase with fresh flowers in it smashed and sprayed shards of ceramic across the room. Above it, a gold-framed mirror exploded when three bullets shattered it.

"In case you can't fucking count, Reaper, we're five floors up."

"I know," Kane said and fired three rounds through the splintered door. "Look, just trust me."

Axe rolled his eyes. "Yeah, right."

Kane gave him a weird smile. "See you down there."

With that, he leaped to his feet and ran for the balcony. Without hesitation, he jumped over the rail. Cara and Axe just looked at the emptiness in disbelief. Axe said, "What the fuck? He's crazy; you know that, right?"

More gunfire ripped through the disintegrating door,

peppering the tastefully decorated room. "I hate that son of a bitch," Cara hissed and started toward the balcony.

Axe called to her, "Hey, where are you going?"

"Five floors down!"

"Oh shit!" he yelled after her as she disappeared. "This is not happening."

Finally, the door gave way and left a gaping hole, the space immediately filled by one of the Black Shield shooters. Axe fired three rounds at him and came to his feet. With his head down, he ran hard for the balcony, bullets flying all around him.

"I have only one thing to say to you, Reaper!" he shouted. *"Fuck yooooouuuu!"*

They seemed to fall forever. A heart-stopping freefall which was only arrested once they hit the crystal-clear waters of the pool below. Luckily for them, and others, there was no one in it.

Breaking the surface, Axe looked up at Kane who was already on the side of the pool. "I hate you, you son of a bitch."

"You're still alive, aren't you?" Kane asked with a smile.

Axe snorted water and watched Kane pull Cara from the pool. Then the team leader looked up and saw the Black Shield operators leaning out over the balcony rail. Without taking his eyes off them, he said, "Get out of the pool, Axe. We need to move. Cara, lead us out the front."

It was like flicking a switch, and all three went back into serious mode. As they walked back through the hotel lobby, people stopped and stared. Maybe it had something to do with the river of water pouring from their saturated clothing, that they were leaving behind them. Kane said in a low voice, "We'll have to get Slick to hack their system and erase all of their security footage."

Cara said, "You're right. I must look terrible."

"You look all right from where I'm standing," Axe said from behind her.

Cara rolled her eyes. "Really? Is that all you think about?"

"Not always."

They exited the hotel and saw Thurston parked across the street. Starting across, they were distracted by the screech of tires. It seemed that Black Shield weren't done with them just yet.

A black SUV pulled away from the curb and came toward them, accelerating hard as it went. Kane stopped and drew his M17, hoping that even wet, it would fire and not blow up in his hand. He fired four shots and watched them punch through the windshield. Beside him, Cara and Axe did the same. Eventually, the SUV swerved and plowed into a parked car.

With the vehicle out of action, they continued to where Thurston was parked. They climbed in, Reaper in the front. She looked at him and asked, "What the hell happened to you?"

From the back, Axe said, "Asshole made us jump from the fifth floor."

The general raised her eyebrows as she shifted into gear. "Really?"

Kane smiled and gave a shrug. "Seemed like the thing to do at the time. Especially after we were set up like we were."

"You're right about that," Thurston snapped. "Someone's going to get reamed over this one."

———

BLACK SHIELD OPS CENTER, WASHINGTON, D.C.

Three people watched on as the operation went to shit in front of them on the big screens. The small body-cams on the operators relayed everything back to the ops-center along with the drone they had secretly roving overhead.

Horn shook his head, but when he spoke, there was a hint of admiration in his voice. "I could use people like that."

"Those are my fucking people they're killing!" Ken Drake snapped, watching the SUV pull away from the curb. "Christ, what a fuck up."

Drake turned his back on the screens in disgust. He was a small man, no taller than five-seven. Somewhere in his forties, he'd come up through the CIA intelligence ranks beside Horn. That was until he'd made his suspicious fortune confiscating money from secret terrorist bank accounts, then branched out on his own. Now he was one of the richest men in the world and stood on the doorstep of a new venture worth billions.

He turned to face the third man, Vice-President Jim Forth. "I thought these people were told to stand down. Am I wrong?"

Forth was in his sixties, with gray hair and a deeply-lined face. "I issued orders for them to stay away from the Jiskani situation," he growled. "However, this shootout at the fucking OK Corral is bullshit. What happened to a 'quiet op'? You just attracted attention from across the whole damned country."

"It's fine, the mess will be cleaned up, and everything will go away. The story will be circulated as a drug war."

Horn nodded. "I can have a team fix that. But we still have a window of opportunity to get rid of them."

"How?" Drake asked.

"The motel where they're staying."

Drake inclined his head thoughtfully and said, "OK." Leaning forward he said to one of his op-center technicians, "Have Delta team tasked to the motel. We'll give it one last shot."

WEST COAST MOTEL, EAST LOS ANGELES

"Get changed, your gear packed, and we're out of here," Thurston snapped before she took her cell out of her pocket and hit speed dial.

"Jones."

"We have a situation."

"I'm listening."

Thurston went on to tell him about Black Shield and what had gone down at the hotel. In addition, about the identity of their target, who he really was.

"Christ. Get out of there, Mary. Get on back to El Paso. This is just getting out of hand."

"We're packing as we speak, sir."

"Good. Call me when you land."

"Yes, sir."

Thurston hung up and started to help load the SUV. Once it was done and everyone was ready, they headed toward the door to leave.

Which was when the two Black Shield SUVs sped into the carpark to finish the job.

BLACK SHIELD OPS CENTER, WASHINGTON, D.C.

"Delta Team arriving onsite."

The voice over the speakers filled the room as they watched the SUVs swing into the parking lot.

Drake said, "Be careful, Delta One. These assholes can fight. Take no chances. If you see a target, put it down."

"Copy."

They watched on as the vehicles disgorged eight Black Shield operators who took up positions while two of them approached the motel room where their targets were. Over the open comms, Horn could hear Delta One issuing orders to his men.

He reached into his pocket and took out his cell. Punching in a number, a voice came back to him. "Newcomb."

"Where are you?"

"About two blocks out."

Horn turned away from the others and lowered his voice. "Stay back, Mark. This is just all going to shit. I want you to put a special team together and standby. Sometime in the near future, I'm going to need you and your men."

"Yes, sir. I'll get onto it."

The line went dead, and Horn placed the cell back in his pocket. He turned back to look at the screen. Then his prophecy came true.

———

WEST COAST MOTEL, EAST LOS ANGELES

"This is just crazy," Kane snarled, impatience in his voice.

He peered out the window and watched as the operators deployed.

"In case any of you have forgotten," Axe said, "there's no back door to this place."

"Backdoors," Kane said.

"I count eight," Cara said.

"I concur," Thurston agreed.

"Bit of a bastard with all our gear packed in the SUV," Kane pointed out.

"You got a plan, Reaper?" Cara asked.

"Working on it."

"I've had enough of this shit," Thurston snarled. "These pricks have pissed me off for the last time."

"Front door, ma'am?" Kane asked.

"Damned right. If I'm going down, it will be fighting."

Thurston's cell rang. She took it from her pocket and looked at the screen. Hitting the answer button, she said, "I'm a bit busy at the moment, Luis."

"I realize that, Mary. We've been monitoring your progress from back here in ops. You've got a DEA Special Response Team perhaps three minutes out. I figured that after the hotel fiasco I'd pull a few strings and have something on standby just in case. You need to hold on until then."

Thurston felt a sudden release of pressure. "Thanks, Luis. I owe you one."

"Keep your head down, Mary."

"Listen up. Our guardian angel has a DEA Special Response Team about three minutes out. We just have to hang in until then."

"We have two men approaching the door," Axe said in a low voice.

Kane glanced back out the window at the two figures.

He set his jaw firm and brought his M17 up. "Prepare for incoming," he snapped. Then he opened fire.

The foremost Black Shield operator fell to the ground in a pool of blood. His friend joined him a moment later with a bullet in his head from Axe.

The front of the motel seemed to explode as the rest of the operators opened fire. Glass shattered as 5.56 rounds from the shooter's CQBRs punched through the windows not already broken. They hammered into the walls as Kane, and the others took cover on the floor.

"You just had to fire, didn't you?" Cara shouted above the din.

"Beats getting shot. Besides, didn't you hear? Help's on the way."

The light-fitting in the center of the room erupted and sprayed glass across the room. "Help is no good if you're dead!" Axe shouted.

Thurston shook her head. This lot would be staring down the barrel of a gun and, they'd still be cool and calm.

"Hey, General. Buy you a drink later after we're done here?" Reaper shouted across to her.

Gunfire smashed the lamp next to one of the beds. Thurston ducked and then called out, "It'll have to wait until we get home. Then I'll buy you all one."

"OK. But –"

"Ah, shit!" Cara exclaimed. "One of them has a two-oh-three."

An M203 grenade launcher put a whole new spin on things. Fire one of those things through the window, and in the close confines of the room, they were all screwed.

"We've gotta put him down," Kane snapped as he came to his feet in a bold move. Axe followed suit, and both blew off the rest of their magazines in the attempt to take the shooter out.

Both ran dry, and the operator with the 203 was still alive, down behind the engine block of an SUV. "Damn it," Kane cursed.

Cara rose and fired two shots before dropping again. She shouted at Kane. "So, it's true!"

"What?"

"You two can't shoot for shit."

Kane slapped a fresh magazine home and rose once more to fire at the man with the 203. He needn't have worried. Cara had put him down with the last burst she fired.

———

BLACK SHIELD OPS CENTER, WASHINGTON, D.C.

Horn shook his head as he watched Delta Team die one by one. They'd started with eight shooters, and now they were down to four.

"Christ, Delta One! What the fuck are you doing?" Drake snarled into his comms.

The team leader said something, but through the din of the gunfire, Horn couldn't make out his reply.

"Sir, we have two vehicles inbound!" one of the technicians said in a loud voice. A picture appeared on a different screen. Two Humvees.

"Looks like backup is on the way," Horn observed. "Get your people out of there, Ken, or you'll lose them all."

"We've almost got them."

"No, you haven't. Get them out; we've lost."

"Damn it," Drake cursed. Then, "Delta One, break contact. I say again, break contact. They've got reinforcements on the way."

The speakers crackled. "Copy. Delta Team is breaking contact."

WEST COAST MOTEL, EAST LOS ANGELES

"They're bugging out," Cara said as the Black Shield operators piled into their armored SUVs.

The noise of the shooting died away and was replaced by the roar of engines and the squeal of tires as the vehicles tore out of the carpark, leaving the dead in their wake.

The Team Reaper members slowly emerged from the shattered motel room and out into the blazing sun. Four bodies lay in the lot, pools of blood around them. Thurston turned to look back at the façade of the motel. It was riddled with bullet holes. She turned back at the sound of revving engines. Two Humvees appeared, roaring into the parking lot. Armed men spilled out and took up defensive positions.

One, a tall man dressed in tactical gear, walked across to them. He studied the motel façade and said, "Looks like you folks have had some trouble."

Thurston shook her head. "Not really. Just another day."

CHAPTER 7

TEAM REAPER HQ, EL PASO, TEXAS—ONE WEEK LATER

"YOU'VE GOT TO BE KIDDING," Axe blurted out. "That's it? That little fucker kills my sister and gets away with it."

There were four of them in Thurston's office. The general, Ferrero, Kane, and Axe. But the voice that had spoken wasn't one of theirs. It emanated from a speaker on Thurston's desk phone.

"What I'm saying is that you will all stand down," Jones' voice filled the room, deep, commanding. "This is a whole lot more complicated than was first thought."

"Seems pretty simple from where I'm standing, General," Axe snapped.

"The order has come down from the vice-president," Jones said, his voice calm.

"Sorry, General," Kane interrupted. "But you know he's tied up in this too?"

"Yes, damn it, Gunny. I do," Jones snapped.

"Well, what are you doing about it?" Axe snarled.

"Stand down, marine," Jones demanded. Even though he could understand Axe's anger, he was only willing to let him take it so far.

"What are we to do then?" Thurston asked, interrupting.

"Nothing. Just go about doing what you do."

"Excuse me, General," Ferrero said.

"What is it, Luis?"

"Sir, our computer tech has been doing some digging around into Marek and his son," Ferrero continued. "This guy is up to his eyeballs in something illegal. I think the story that the gang leader told us about them supplying drugs could be true."

"It doesn't change the fact, Luis, that he is the Polish Minister of Defense and is the linchpin to a billion-dollar deal which involves the biggest donor to the president's election campaign."

"The same people who tried to kill us," Kane pointed out. "Have you seen the video, sir?"

"I have."

"And?"

"Without more evidence, it's just that. A video. They could dismiss it by saying it was doctored."

"Shit," Axe swore.

Jones ignored it and continued, "However, I'm still looking into it and all of the other bullshit which has been going on. Just keep your heads down."

"Yes, sir. Thank you, sir," Thurston said and hung up.

The silence which ensued was broken by Axe. "That's fucking bullshit. We all know it."

"You heard the general, Axel," Thurston's voice grew hard. "We are to stand down. Take a few days off, and get your head around things."

Axe lifted his chin in defiance. "Is that an order, ma'am?"

"No, a suggestion. But if you wish me to make it one, then I can."

"Fine," Axe growled and turned, storming out of the office.

"He's right, ma'am," Kane said.

"Of course, he's fucking right," Thurston swore savagely. "And it grates against every bone in my damned body to let it go. But that is just what we'll do. Understood?"

"Yes, ma'am."

———

TEAM REAPER HQ, EL PASO, TEXAS

Four days later Kane knocked on Thurston's door, a worried expression on his face. She took one look at him and knew something was wrong. "What is it?"

"Axe has disappeared," he said.

"What do you mean, disappeared?"

"I went to see him, and he's gone. The bed hasn't been slept in, clothes are missing, and I checked to see if I could find his passport and came up empty."

Concern was etched on the general's face. "You don't think...?"

"I don't know, ma'am."

"God, I hope we're wrong," she said and came up out of her chair. "On me."

Kane followed her out into the operations room where they found Swift. The redhead was sitting at his station, looking at something on the screen. Thurston said, "Slick, you got a moment?"

He spun around. "Yes, ma'am."

Reynolds, Teller, and Ferrero were also in the room and stared in their direction when they heard the tone of their commander's voice. She said, "I want you to check any outgoing flights over the past few days and look for Axe's name on the flight manifest."

"Yes, ma'am," he said and spun back around.

"Do we have a problem, Mary?" Ferrero asked as he approached.

She looked up at him. "I pray not, Luis."

It didn't take long. A few minutes later Swift had what they wanted. He put it on the big screen. "There, ma'am."

Highlighted on the screen amongst a list of names was one Axel Burton.

"Damn it," Thurston hissed. "Do I have to guess where he's gone?"

"No, ma'am. The flight's destination was Europe. To be more precise, Warsaw, Poland."

"Christ."

"This is bad," Ferrero said. "You can bet Black Shield know where he is. And if they do, there's no way in hell that they'll let him get close to his intended target. They'll kill him, for sure."

"If they don't know," Thurston said. "They soon will. Damn it, I need to talk to General Jones."

———

LANGLEY, VIRGINIA

Paul Horn stood at the plate-glass window and stared outward at the forest. The day was drab-gray, with rain tumbling down, small rivulets of water sliding down the glass, obscuring part of his view. Clouds hung low like a dense mist. That very same view earlier in the day had been clear of everything. Even the sky had been clear of the gray beasts which dumped their excess condensation.

The office was a large space. When Horn had first moved into the office, the walls had been wood-paneled. Since the renovations, the office was white. There were a few pictures on the walls, a couple of chairs, and one solitary artificial plant in the corner. Just the way Horn wanted it. Any files he required were kept in a storage space behind the wall along with other things. A button on his desk opened a hidden door which was quite well camouflaged.

The phone on his hardwood desk buzzed, drawing his attention. Horn walked across to it and pressed one of the buttons on it. "Yes?"

"Deputy Director, an envelope just arrived for you. It has urgent marked on it."

"Thank you, Naomi. Bring it in, please."

A few moments later, the thick wood door opened, and a young lady in her twenties walked in holding a yellow A4 envelope. She handed it across to Horn who took it and said, "Thank you."

"Welcome, sir." She left, closing the door behind her.

Horn held the envelope in one hand and picked up an antique letter opener from beside a tin full of pens. He used it then lay it back down, emptying the contents onto his desk. Three things came out. Two were photos, black and white, but clear. The third was a piece of paper with a message printed on it.

The deputy director read the message first. Frowning, he then picked up the photos. They looked to be stills from different security cameras. One was in an airport. The other looked to be from a street camera.

"Son of a bitch," he muttered and checked the time stamps. He'd arrived in Warsaw the day before, which meant he could only be there for one reason. Horn pulled his cell from his pocket.

"Hello," Newcomb said.

"Mark, you and your team are flying out to Poland today. I'll send you the details."

"What's up?"

"I need you to kill someone. I'll also phone ahead and let them know you're coming."

"You got it."

The line went dead. Horn was studying the pictures when his cell buzzed. He answered it. The person on the other end was Drake. "We have a problem."

"What is it?" Horn asked.

"Hank Jones is doing some digging behind the scenes. He needs to be stopped, or this will all fall through, and I'll lose billions. And if I lose that, you'll lose the thirty million I'm paying you."

"I'll have someone take care of it."

Make sure you do."

Horn hung up and took out a second cell. He dialed another number. This one went through to a burner phone. "Yes?"

"I have a job for you."

"How much?"

"Two million."

There was silence at the other end of the line.

"Are you still there?"

"Yes. It must be a high-value target?"

"Put it this way. Once it's done, you'll need to get out of the country."

"OK."

"I'll put the folder in the usual drop."

"When?"

"This afternoon."

"I'll be expecting it."

TEAM REAPER HQ, EL PASO, TEXAS

"What a crock of shit this has turned into, Mary," Hank Jones snapped.

"I'm sorry, sir, it's my fault. He's my guy."

"No, Mary. Don't blame yourself. This was put into action long before your man got on that plane."

"Thank you, General."

"OK, listen up. Get your team packed up and on a blasted C-17. Once you get on board, give me a call."

"Where are we going?"

"Ramstein. By the time you arrive, I will have organized with them to have somewhere for you to set up."

"Um, that's not Warsaw, sir."

"No. You're not going to Warsaw. You, along with a majority of your team, will hold at Ramstein. You'll send Reaper and the others to Warsaw. They'll find your man and get out."

"We can't be much help to them a thousand kilometers away, sir."

"You'll make do. If there's trouble, you'll have to find a place for them to hole up. We've a few safehouses there."

"I don't like it, sir."

"I'm afraid, Mary, it's all you're going to get."

"Yes, sir."

He sensed disapproval in her tone. "I'm sorry, Mary, but it has to be this way."

"Yes, sir."

"If you need any help, there's a team of Air Commandos at Ramstein on R&R. Second them if you need to."

"Yes, sir."

"Call me when you get in the air."

The line went dead, and Thurston pressed a button on her phone. Ferrero answered it, and she said, "You and Reaper. My office."

A few minutes later they stood before her desk. "Get everything packed up. We're headed to Ramstein. Reaper, work out a plan to get you and your team into Poland and then out again. Preferably without anyone knowing about it."

"What assets will we have, ma'am?" Kane asked.

"We'll have to get some wheels for you over there. Also, you'll need a way to get weapons across the border. Handguns only. If you need your 416s, the mission's screwed. Bravo elements will direct everything from Ramstein."

"Any air assets, ma'am?"

"No."

"What about backup if we need it?"

"Apparently there are some Air Commandos at the base. We can use them if need be."

"That's a long haul."

"We'll have them stationed close to the border."

"I still don't like it."

"Neither do I. Get your people ready."

———

PENTAGON, WASHINGTON, D.C.

The phone on Jones' desk rang, and he cursed under his breath. The last thing he needed was an interruption. He picked it up and snapped, "Jones!"

The call was short, the voice electronically distorted. "Your man has a termination order on him. Get him out."

"Who is this?" Jones demanded.

The line went dead.

————

BIGGS AIRFIELD, OUTSIDE EL PASO

Biggs Army Airfield began its life in 1915 as part of Fort Bliss. It was home to the Texas 82nd Field Artillery. Since then it had played host to the 94th Bombardment Group in '42, the 392nd in '43, as well as the 389th.

In 1966 it was closed, only to be re-opened in 1973 as a permanent U.S. Army Airfield. In '90 to '91, Biggs Army Airfield supported the airlift for Operations' Desert Shield and Storm.

With 4,138 meters of runway and 15.6 kilometers of taxiway, it was more than capable of handling the C-17 Globemaster.

The plane had a cruising speed of 829 kilometers per hour. Which meant that with its current light load, it could make the journey to Ramstein without refueling. Only four hours had elapsed between Jones hanging up and the last of the team's equipment being loaded onto the Globemaster.

Thurston turned to Kane. She was dressed in fatigue pants and a dark green t-shirt. The rest of the team were dressed the same way. It was done that way, so they didn't look out of place on the airbase.

Thurston opened her mouth to speak, but the scream of an F-15E drowned out her words. She paused, and as the fighter's roar died away over the desert, she tried again. "Do you have everything you need?"

He nodded. "Yes, ma'am."

"Good. What about Cara? All armaments and associated equipment aboard?"

"Yes."

Ferrero approached them at the head of the ramp of the giant transport. "Luis, do your people have everything?"

He nodded. "I think so."

"All right then. Let's get this bird in the air. I've just got to call the general. Let the captain know we're ready to roll."

"Will do," Ferrero said.

"Reaper, before you go, while we're in the air, have Brick make up a small medical kit to take with you into Poland. There's no cause for him to be carrying a Unit One pack."

"I'll let him know."

"Good. Dismissed."

Once Kane was gone, she reached into her pocket and called Jones on her cell. When he answered, he told her of the call he'd received earlier. "Any idea who it was, sir?"

"No clue, Mary. Which means you'll have to find your boy as soon as possible."

"It has to be them," Thurston stated.

"Black Shield? Maybe. Or it is the CIA. Whoever it is, you can be sure that they'll have more than enough boots on the ground to get the job done."

"What's our cover story, General?"

"You're over there to escort an HVT back to the U.S. for trial," Jones explained.

"Really. Will it fly?"

"It'll fly to the moon and back because the Germans have Fabian Falk in custody."

"*The* Fabian Falk? The meth manufacturer? Since when?"

"Since yesterday. He was picked up in a random traffic stop if you can believe that? Just like the damned movies. So, while your boys are in Poland, you'll send someone to interrogate him. Got it?"

"Yes, sir."

"Good. Touch base when you land. And good luck, Mary."

"Thank you, sir."

Thurston hung up the phone and turned away from the ramp. She walked into the belly of the beast, its giant jaws swallowing her.

———

WARSAW POLAND, CLUB 27

Axe knew that he was doing the wrong thing. But at that point in time, he didn't give two shits either way. Since landing in Warsaw, his entire focus had been on finding Bazyli Marek. Hell, it had been all he could think about since Remy's murder. Now, he was all but there. If his intel was good, the bastard would be here. He stood at the base of Level 27 Nightclub and looked up.

The club itself was located on the 28th and 32nd floors of the Spectrum Tower in the heart of Warsaw. The 32nd floor was the rooftop bar, with 360-degree panoramic views and room for almost five hundred people. There was a DJ booth, circular bar, twenty-eight tables with sofas providing seating for two hundred. On the 28th floor was another bar, the dance floor, and DJ booth, and two terraced area with tables and sofas, the first of which had a fireplace, the other, a fountain.

Axe looked at the line of would-be patrons on the street, queued at the door to the elevators. On either side stood two large security guards. As each person stepped up to the entry, their identification was checked, and they were either granted access to the inner sanctum or refused and turned away. Well, he sure as hell wasn't going to join the back of the line. After all, it stretched down around the block.

Head down, Axe approached the doors. One of the security men stepped in front of him and said, "*Gdzie się wybierasz?*"

Axe stared at him. "What?"

"Where are you going?" he asked, changing to heavily-accented English.

"I have an appointment with someone upstairs," Axe told him.

The security man shook his bald head. "*Nie.*"

He didn't need an interpreter to know what the man had said. Axe tried again. "I have an appointment."

The man opened his jacket and flashed what looked to be a WIST-94, 9mm handgun. He raised his eyebrows and held Axe's gaze. Cursing inwardly Axe tried to work out what to do next. It was then that the security guy's partner finished chatting to a couple of young ladies and came across to see what was happening.

"*Co się dzieje?*" the thick-set man asked, eyeing Axe suspiciously.

The pair rattled off a few more words in Polish, and then the newcomer did something which set Axe on edge.

He reached inside his coat. The ex-recon marine braced himself as the security man eased his hand free of the flap. But instead of a handgun, he had a picture. He showed it to his friend, and they both stared at Axe before looking at it again. The first man said something that Axe didn't understand, but when he moved, his intentions were clear.

Before the security guard's hand could touch his weapon, Axe closed in and brought his right elbow up and around. The blow was solid, and the force of it reverberated up Axe's arm into his shoulder. He was almost certain he'd broken the guy's jaw but didn't really give a damn. That would teach him for reaching for his gun.

The second man reacted the same way, going for a concealed weapon. Axe drew his right arm back and punched him in the middle of the face. The man reeled back, and Axe followed. The ex-recon marine landed two more fast blows which knocked the man to the sidewalk, stunned.

The gasps of the onlookers began to grow into concerned yelps. Axe ignored them and reached for the fallen picture. He flipped it over and saw his face staring back at him. They knew he was here. Someone had tipped them off.

He bent down again and opened the first man's coat, reaching inside for the WIST-94. Searching next for fresh magazines, he found two in an inner pocket. Straightening up, he glanced around then ran across the street, leaving the shocked onlookers following him with their bemused gazes and phone cameras.

CHAPTER 8

RAMSTEIN AIRFORCE BASE, GERMANY

THE C-17 TOUCHED down in Ramstein, Germany at approximately midday after the long flight. The day was warm, and the skies clear. There was an abundance of air traffic on the tarmac, and it looked like a medical flight had landed shortly before them; a C-17 visible with its ramp down and an ambulance backed up to it.

The whole team was dressed in civilian attire when they walked down the ramp. There to meet them were an officer and two Humvee drivers, allocated for their use.

The officer walked up to Thurston and asked, "Are you General Thurston, ma'am?"

"I am."

He went to salute her, but her arm shot out and stopped him. "We'll let that go, shall we?"

The officer was confused but nodded. "Yes, ma'am. I'm Captain Richards, ma'am. I've been designated to show you to your operations quarters."

"Thank you. What about our things?"

"A truck will be here shortly, and they will be loaded with everything you require."

"Thank you. Lead the way, Captain."

Both teams walked toward the Humvees. Reaper looked about the base as he went, Cara walking beside him. "How long since you were here last, Reaper?"

"Been a while. You?"

"Same."

They climbed into the vehicles and were transported to a hangar at the edge of the airfield. The structure was large with huge double doors at the front, which were closed. They gained access via an alternate opening. Once inside, the team found that there were already bunks set up for them, housed in a prefab enclosure with plastic for walls and nothing on the ceiling. It looked more like open dog kennels than bunk space.

"Sorry about the lack of privacy, ma'am," Richards apologized. "But it's all we have at this point. Showers and toilets are two buildings back along, ma'am."

"I'm sure it will all be fine, Captain," Thurston reassured him. "I have people going to interrogate an important HVT tomorrow. Has transport been organized for them?"

"That won't be necessary, ma'am. The detainee in question was moved here onto the base by German authorities."

"OK. That's something," the general said. Then, "How much have you been told about why we're here, Captain?"

"General Jones filled me in, ma'am."

"So, you know that I am sending a team into Warsaw?"

"Yes, ma'am. There will be a Black Hawk waiting on the tarmac tonight. It will fly your people closer to the

Polish border where there will be a car waiting for them. From there, they're on their own."

Thurston nodded. "Thank you."

"If there is nothing else, ma'am, I'll see to the unloading of your equipment."

"Since we're going to be working together, Captain Richards, maybe you should tell me your first name."

"Jacob, ma'am."

"OK, Jacob. Just one more thing. We're not strict on formalities inside our team. So, you can loosen up a little."

"Yes, ma'am."

Richards excused himself, and Kane walked over to Thurston and asked, "What's news, ma'am?"

"A Black Hawk has been organized for tonight to drop you close to the Polish border. You'll take Brick and Carlos with you. I want Cara to stay here with me where she and Pete can interrogate Falk."

"Who's Falk?"

"Big-time meth manufacturer. He's here on base. The Germans picked him up. He's the *reason* we're here. I am almost certain that due to the nature of his work throughout Europe, he would have had some dealings or at least contact with Gustaw Marek."

"I thought we weren't here after that Marek?"

"We're not."

"Cara won't like it," Kane pointed out.

"That's my decision."

"Yes, ma'am."

"Once the gear is unloaded, gather everything you'll need. I'll have Slick put together all the intel he has, and we'll run through it before wheels up."

"I'll get it done."

Thurston walked away and sought out Ferrero, leaving Kane deep in thought.

"What's up?"

Kane turned to face Cara. "The general was just giving me a rundown of some of the operation."

"Such as?"

"You'll be staying here with Traynor."

"What?"

Kane winced when he saw the expression on her face. He held up a hand in defense and said, "Easy. Just listen. You and Pete will be interrogating a meth manufacturer named Falk. Thurston thinks he might have some intel on Marek."

"Shit," Cara hissed. "I hate being sidelined."

"I understand. But if you can glean something useful, then it's worth it."

"OK. But you owe me."

He smiled at her. "I'll always owe you."

———

WARSAW-MODLIN AIRPORT, POLAND

The Gulfstream G650 touched down at Warsaw-Modlin Airport almost two hours after Team Reaper landed in Ramstein. It taxied to a private hangar where it was met by four dark blue Peugeot 3008 SUVs. Nine men and a woman exited the plane, each carrying their own kit.

A man in his mid-thirties approached from one of the Peugeots. "Mr. Newcomb?"

"Yes."

"My name is Leon. I am here to take you to see Minister Marek."

Newcomb nodded. "Fine. Has there been accommodation arranged for us?"

"*Tak.* Yes. I am to take you to see the minister, and the

rest are to be taken to where you will be staying. After which, the drivers will leave the cars with your men."

Again, Newcomb nodded. He signaled to one of his team; a big, broad-shouldered operator with a bald head and beard. He walked over to Newcomb and stopped in front of him. "Hank, go with the drivers. They'll take you to where we're staying. When you get there get everything setup and operational. I want our business accomplished as soon as possible."

"Yes, sir," Hank Greer replied and turned away to organize the rest of the team.

The CIA man had chosen his people well. Some, like Greer were ex-Delta. A few of the others had been SEALS in a previous life, and one had been a Ranger. All had worked black ops for the CIA Special Activities division in the past and seen plenty of action. They also knew what was expected of them and would do so without question.

"Am I going with them?" Nicole asked her boss.

"No, you're with me. Put your bag in the SUV with Hank Greer. Bring your sidearm, though."

"Yes, sir."

"The minister said for you to come alone," Leon reminded Newcomb.

The CIA man shrugged. "I'm sure he'll get over it."

---

27 ULICA WILLIAM, WARSAW, POLAND

The meeting place was a huge, old-style double-story mansion with triangular-pitched roofs and surrounded by trees and gardens. The lawn was well-manicured, and the gravel drive ended into a turnaround at the house itself.

Entry was gained through a pair of automatic, wrought-iron gates.

Wide steps led up to a broad cement landing with ceramic pots filled with flowering plants scattered at regular intervals.

Leon stopped the vehicle and climbed out. While Newcomb did the same, Leon walked around to the rear door on the passenger side, his shoes crunching on the gravel. He opened the door for Nicole to exit. As she did, he noticed how her skirt rode up her thigh and let his gaze linger longer than was appropriate. When she caught him staring, the man turned red with embarrassment, but Nicole only smiled and pulled her hem back down to a respectable level.

"If you will follow me," he said.

They walked up the steps to a large wooden door with exposed brass hinges fixed to it. Leon opened it, and they walked through into a cavernous reception area which reminded them both of the grand entrances on old black and white movies of yesteryear. Except this one was in full color, and the magnificence was real. The wide stairway that rose majestically to the second level had marble steps that matched the floor, the detailed pattern matching the fretwork on the balustrades. A chandelier hung from a vaulted ceiling decorated with ornate cornicing. The exterior of the home had given no indication of the opulence that lay within.

"I could get used to something like this," Nicole murmured.

"Only if you do what he does," Newcomb said.

"This way," Leon said, leading them through to a set of double doors. Rapping briskly on the door, he didn't wait for an answer before swinging one open, entering, then stepping aside. They followed him through, and he closed the door behind them.

If the entrance had been designed to wow, the library was just an overindulgence of money. It was a picture of bookshelves and ornate woodwork which took up not one, but two floors. The intervening ceiling had been removed and around the wall was a walkway with fretted railing. It divided two large mullioned windows which were designed to make the most of the daylight. An open wood fire was embedded into the west wall and above it hung a large painting of Frederick Chopin.

The furniture was all handcrafted, from luxurious sofas, chairs, and tables, to the lavish desk made from hard-to-get Cocobolo wood from Central America.

"Holy shit," Nicole breathed. "Imagine dusting all this."

"*Imponujące, czyż nie?*" a man seated in one of the sumptuous handmade chairs said as he stood up.

Newcomb stared blankly at him. It was Nicole who said, "Yes, very impressive."

The man chuckled. "I'm sorry. It is something I do when foreigners come to my home," he said, switching to near-flawless English. "I am Gustaw Marek."

Marek wasn't a big man by any means. He was of average build with graying hair and a face which was starting to age. Nicole figured him to be in his early fifties.

The CIA man nodded. "I am Mark Newcomb. This is Nicole Cresswell."

Marek indicated a couple of seats. "Please, take one. Would either of you like a drink?"

Newcomb shook his head. "No, thank you, Mr. Marek. We'd like to get down to business if that's all right with you?"

Marek's expression changed. "Yes, business."

"You were contacted about the target being in Warsaw, Mr. Marek?" Newcomb asked.

"Yes. As it turned out, the warning was good."

The CIA man leaned forward. "Really? He's attempted to contact your son already?"

Marek nodded. "Yes. My son was at a club he frequents. Club 27 it is called. Your man almost killed the two security guards they have on the main doors at the bottom of the building. It was lucky they had a picture with which they used to recognize him."

"Not for them," Nicole said in a soft voice.

Marek studied her and then nodded. "Yes, true."

"Now that my team and I are here, we should be able to clean up this mess and get back on our plane and home in no time."

"Yes. A most unfortunate set of circumstances. Perhaps if I offer to pay the man some remuneration, he might be happy with that? Do you think?"

"Our way would be best, Mr. Marek," Newcomb said. "Your, son. Is he sequestered away somewhere under armed security?"

"Yes. I've sent him to a secure facility in Latvia with a team of former *Jednostka Wojskowa Komandosów*," he informed them. The *Jednostka Wojskowa Komandosów* happened to be Poland's oldest special forces unit.

"A secure facility?" Nicole questioned.

"That's right."

"What kind of facility?"

"One that you need not worry yourself about," Marek said abruptly.

"Mr. Marek, there are rumors about your business practices. Your other business practices..."

Marek cut her off. "I'm sure, Mr. Newcomb, that it is in everybody's interest that a satisfactory outcome to this matter is reached quickly and efficiently?"

The veiled threat was there as plain as the nose on the old bastard's face. Get the job done and ask no questions, especially about things that didn't concern them. Newcomb said, "Yes, Mr. Marek. I'm sure it is."

"Excellent. I hope you find the accommodations and transport with which I have supplied you, adequate. Goodbye."

And that was that. Meeting over. The CIA man rose to his feet and said, "Goodbye, Mr. Marek."

On their way out through the reception area, Leon met them. He gave Newcomb the keys to the Peugeot and said, "The route is programmed into the navigation system. Also, I have this." He reached into his pocket and took out a burner cell. "It has one number in it. Mine. If you need anything, you should call."

They walked out to the SUV, and Newcomb gave Nicole the keys. "You drive."

Once inside, she started it and slipped the shift into drive. As they pulled away from the house, she said, "Is it true?"

"You know it is, so why ask?"

"So why work with him? He's one of the biggest drug producers in Europe. I'm surprised that he's even able to serve in the Polish government."

"Money and power will take you a long way in this world. You know that. As for working with him, it's the lesser of two evils. Besides, it's what we do. We work in the dark, remember. We do what they tell us to do."

"But still..."

"Are you growing a conscience on me, Nicole? I find it rather tiresome, and I'm afraid it's a bit late for that now."

"No, I'm fine."

"Good. Because the quicker we get this done, the quicker we get to return home."

CHAPTER 9

RAMSTEIN AIRFORCE BASE, GERMANY

KANE CHECKED his equipment and made sure he had everything in his go bag, including spare magazines for the SIG M-17. Beside him, Brick Peters double-checked his medical supplies before zipping up the carrier.

Across from Kane, Arenas was doing the same, checking his weapon and other equipment, as it was too far to come back in case something vital was forgotten. He looked up after zipping his bag and stared at Kane. "I think that is everything, Amigo."

Had anyone else said that sentence with the word think in it, Kane would have questioned their preparedness. But Arenas had been a commander of a Mexican special forces team and was as reliable and professional as they came. A smile split his square jaw. "I have never been to Poland before."

Kane asked, "How about Germany?"

"No."

"Europe?"

"No."

"Where have you been?" Brick asked him.

"America."

Brick shook his head. "Shit."

Arenas laughed out loud and winked at Kane who laughed too. Then he said, "All right. Game faces on. Let's get ready to fly out of here. The general has a briefing for us."

Their briefing room was an open space in the hangar where they gathered around a table with a map and pictures on it. Ferrero, Swift, Thurston, and Cara were already there going over things.

"What do we have, ma'am?" Kane asked.

"OK. You'll be wheels up within the hour. The Black Hawk will take you to the designated LZ, and that's where you'll pick up a vehicle. From there, you'll make your way over the border and into Warsaw. The DIA has a safehouse that you can operate out of unless things change. Remember, this is a retrieval operation only. You find Axe and get him out of there. That is it. Be aware. You will not be the only ones looking for him. Before we left El Paso, I had a call from General Jones informing me of a termination order on Axe's head."

Kane cursed softly. "Any prizes for guessing who put it there, ma'am?"

"I guess not. Although, I've had Slick working his magic, and he came up with something for us."

Reaper shifted his gaze, and Swift cleared his throat. "I did some digging and came up with a Gulfstream that landed in Poland a couple of hours after we touched down in Ramstein. It originated from Washington. A small airfield which our friendly neighborhood spooks like to use when they want to remain out of sight. I even managed to get us some happy snaps."

Swift pushed a couple of pictures across the table, and Kane picked the first one up. He studied the picture and asked, "How did you get this?"

Swift smiled. "The miracles of modern technology, my friend."

Kane tossed it back on the table. The picture was grainy and black and white. There was no question about the identities of the pair. One was Nicole, or Iona as he'd known her. The other was the killer from the CIA, Newcomb. "It looks like their team has already arrived."

Thurston nodded, face grim. "Yes, which means that it's imperative that you find Axe as fast as you can."

"I hate to point this out, ma'am, but it's a big-ass city."

"That's where Slick comes in. He's managed to find a satellite we can use, and he'll be able to hack into city cameras and see if we can pick up anything on facial recognition."

"You might want to put Newcomb's face in the search too," Kane suggested. "Just in case they pick up something before we do."

"Already doing it," Thurston informed him. "I want two-hourly check-ins. If you miss one, and I mean just one, I'll spin up our QRF."

Kane frowned. "QRF?"

"Myself and Cara. And I don't believe you'll all be too happy with a couple of chicks pulling your asses out of the fire. So, might I suggest that you keep them out of it?"

"Copy. What happened to our air commandos?"

"Forget about them. Any questions?"

"No, ma'am."

"OK, gentlemen, good luck."

Ferrero said to Kane, "Reaper, we can't stress enough how dangerous this is. The CIA are going to throw everything they have at this. If they get wind of your team, you can guarantee they will come after you too. The only unknown fact is what Marek brings to the table."

"Don't worry, Luis. We'll watch our sixes."

"Make sure you do."

———

WARSAW BACKPACKERS HOSTEL, WARSAW, POLAND

A loose floorboard. The thing Axe would remember most about the backpacker's dive he was staying in, was the loose floorboard. For the simple fact that it saved his life. He was laying on his back on the bed, a spring from the lumpy mattress digging into his back. He was still fully clothed, something he'd gotten used to in the Corps. Be ready for anything.

Axe's eyes were closed as he worked on a strategy for the following day. They knew he was here so that meant they would send the son of a bitch Marek underground. He just needed to know where.

Since he'd been in Poland, he'd done his own recon. That was how he knew the asshole who killed his sister was at the place called Club 27. He also had laid eyes on the father and knew that he had a driver take him everywhere he went. He would be the next target. Get the driver and question him. If anyone knew Gustaw Marek's business, it would be him.

Wondering whether the team knew he was in Poland, he was reasonably certain that they did, considering Slick's skillset. Well, he could kiss that avenue of work goodbye.

Outside, a car horn blasted. It was answered by another, more tinny-sounding one. That was the trouble with sleeping on the second floor of a backpacker's hovel in the middle of a city. Apart from all the backpackers and their six or seven different languages, the bedbugs from the constant turnover of clientele, sharing a bathroom, or small kitchen for that fact, it was the street noise that echoed off the paved streets and upward.

Suddenly the couple in the room next door started up. Paper-thin walls provided no insulation against their moans and other various sounds of passion. This was followed by the banging of the bed's headboard against the wall.

Axe sighed and sat up. He swung his legs over the edge of the bed and looked around the box he was bunked in. A dim light filtered through the window from the street outside. Two of the three other bunkbeds were occupied, both by males. One was Swedish, the other, he thought came from Brazil. That was another drawback. Lack of privacy.

The floorboard outside in the narrow hall squeaked from pressure being exerted on it, and Axe held his breath. Normally when the board squeaked, there was the tell-tale sound of footfalls preceding it as well as afterward. But there was none of that, just the squeak.

He eased his hand under his pillow and found the butt of the WIST-94. He wrapped his fingers around it.

Suddenly the door flew open and crashed back against the wall. The void was filled by a man holding a raised handgun. He stepped into the room to clear the doorway for the next in line. By the time this one appeared, the first had opened fire.

The suppressed weapon coughed twice. The slugs flew harmlessly through empty space and punched into the wall. Axe had sprung into action upon noticing the movement of the door. He raised the WIST-94 and fired twice. The noise of the unsuppressed handgun was almost deafening in the confined space.

The first round thumped into the front shooter's chest. The second took him in the throat and a spray of blood, dark in the dimness of the room, painted the wall closest to the door. Axe shifted his aim to the second shooter and fired again. His shot, however, was too hurried, and it buried into the wood doorframe next to the shooter's head.

Meanwhile, inside the room, the two sleeping backpackers surged to life. Covers were thrown back, and they came to their feet, shouting at the top of their voices. More bullets from the shooter in the doorway flew around the room, and Axe was forced to dive for the floor. The bastard had himself an MP5SD. The fire selector was flicked onto full auto, and he was letting rip with it.

"Get down! Get the fuck down!" Axe shouted at the two young men. A bullet clipped the Brazilian, and he cried out in pain. He spun around and fell to the floor. The Swede didn't need to be told twice. He hit the floor and clamped his hands over his head.

Bullets scythed across the room. Plaster from the paper-thin walls fell in chunks, and white powder filled the air. Axe rolled to the right and bullets hammered into the floor. WHACK! WHACK! WHACK!

"Fuck!" he hissed through clenched teeth. The Wist-94 came up and snapped into line with the shooter. The handgun bucked three times, and the attacker jerked under the impact of each round.

Collapsing to the floor, he spasmed and went still. Axe came to his feet, keeping his weapon trained on the door. "Stay down!" he snapped at the two backpackers. On the floor, the Brazilian squirmed from the pain of his wound.

Axe checked the hallway. It was clear. Throughout

the hostel, things were starting to come alive. He checked the two downed shooters for any signs of life. Both were dead. He dug through their pockets but found nothing. They both had comms, and he was about to rise to his feet when he saw the small camera pinned to the second shooter's shirt. Picking it up, he examined it. He'd seen them before. Hell, he'd used one. That meant these guys weren't Poles; they were American. Things had just gone from the frying pan to deep shit.

———

CIA BLACK OPS BASE, WARSAW, POLAND

Newcomb looked at the face staring back at him. They'd watched the firefight unfold on the laptop. Watched their two-man team die. His jaw set firm as he felt his anger bubble just below the surface.

"Team One is down, sir," a voice said.

"I can see that, damn it," Newcomb growled. "Send Team Two. Tell Greer not to fuck it up."

He heard the team's comms tech say, "Raven Base to Raven One, copy?"

There was a moment's silence, and then the tech said, "Team One is down, Raven One. Orders are to insert Team Two. Base out."

The comms tech turned and said, "Greer and Team Two going in now, sir."

It hadn't taken long for them to track down their target. The tech on the team had managed to hack the city's cameras, and after a while, he'd scored a hit. That was when Newcomb had dispatched his teams. But so far, Axe was proving to be a handful.

Newcomb nodded and glanced sideways at Nicole. "Let's see the fucker get away from this."

———

WARSAW BACKPACKERS HOSTEL, WARSAW, POLAND

Axe examined the Brazilian's wound and found it to be not much more than a scratch. He patted him on the shoulder and said, "You'll be fine."

Then shouts sounded in the distance, followed by the thunder of thudding boots on the stairs. Too slow to be going down, Axe thought. Which meant they were coming up. He hurried to the door and peered around it. While he waited, the noise grew louder. Then it stopped. Suddenly a big man with a bald head and beard appeared at the end of the hall. He carried with him a suppressed MP5.

"Shit," Axe cursed. He ducked back into the room just as the man spotted him and let loose with a burst of fire. He turned to his roommates and shouted at them, "Get under the beds! Now!"

They scrambled under their bunks and disappeared. Axe leaned around the corner and blew off three rounds along the hallway before the slide locked back when the magazine ran dry.

He ducked back and dropped the empty magazine from the WIST-94 and scrambled across to his bag. Digging around inside he promptly found a fresh magazine and slapped it home. He rushed back to the doorway and peered around the jamb. There were three of them, and he could see that all were armed with suppressed MP5s. Their leader caught sight of him and fired a short burst which ripped past, causing Axe to duck back. The bastards had him trapped. He looked down at the WIST and swore. He was outgunned and outmanned.

Time to go. But where? Axe glanced at the window. Shit! Not again. He dropped near the dead guy who'd been armed with the MP5. Picking it up, he also grabbed the spare magazines and tucked them into his bag and retrieved it. He said, "You guys stay under the beds, and you'll be fine. It ain't you they're after."

With that, Axe took a deep breath and ran toward the window. This was going to hurt.

RAMSTEIN AIRFORCE BASE, GERMANY

"Zero, I'm picking up chatter through a *Policja* channel about shots being fired in downtown Warsaw," Swift called out to Ferrero. The *Policja* were the Polish police.

The ex-DEA agent looked down at his watch. It was close to ten p.m. He walked across to where Swift sat and asked, "What can you make of it?"

"I'm not sure, sir."

"Whereabouts in downtown Warsaw, Slick? Can you get an address?"

Swift's fingers danced across the keys of the laptop, and he waited a couple of seconds for it to process and retrieve the information he wanted. "It's a backpacker's hostel."

"All right. See if you can hack into a feed from somewhere. I'll wake up Mary."

"Yes, sir."

Ferrero walked over to Thurston's cage and was about

to rattle it when the voice from within said, "I'm awake, Luis. What is it?"

"It may be nothing, Mary, but it might be something. Warsaw Police are reporting what appears to be a gunfight at a backpacker's hostel."

He heard the cot creak and then the curtain which acted as a door drew back. "Sounds like the kind of place our boy would stay."

"Yes, ma'am. My thoughts exactly. I've got Slick working on getting us a feed."

Then a thought occurred to Thurston. "God, I hope they haven't found him already."

"It's possible."

"Shit!"

Slick was still working on getting a feed up when they reached his work station. "How are we looking, Slick?"

"Almost there. I did find out something else, sir. Another signal. I can't trace it, but someone else is tuned in."

Thurston said in a grim voice, "I guess that answered my question."

"What's up?"

Ferrero turned and saw Cara approaching them. Behind her was Pete Traynor."We could have a situation."

"Axe?"

Ferrero nodded.

"There," Swift said with satisfaction, and on the temporary big screen in front of them, a picture of the hostel appeared, albeit from an elevated angle.

Ferrero pointed at the screen. Down the bottom corner, figures ran from an open doorway, scattering in every direction. If there had been audio, they assumed that the screams would be deafening. "I guess that's the place."

"I've managed to crack that signal, ma'am."

"Bring it up."

A small box at the bottom right of the screen appeared. They stared at it for a moment, and Cara said, "It's a body cam."

A speaker crackled to life. *"Raven One from Raven Base, sitrep over?"*

"They're American," Traynor growled.

"Raven Base, we're taking fire. I say again, we're taking fire."

"Copy."

Suddenly on the big screen, a window on the second floor exploded outward, and something came hurtling through it. The object fell like a stone amongst shards of shattered glass. Cara and the others watched on in horror as it landed on the roof of a vehicle below, blowing out the windows and putting a huge dent in it.

"Holy crap!" Traynor gasped. "Is that...?"

"Yes," murmured Thurston. "It is a body."

Whoever it was, moved. Only marginally, but it was there.

"They're still alive," Ferrero noted.

As they watched, the person moved again. This time it was more pronounced as they tried to roll from the metal depression. The third time they succeeded and hit the sidewalk in an untidy heap. The person staggered to their feet and picked up a bag before limping away. Then whoever it was stopped, turned, and looked up.

"Get that," Thurston snapped.

Swift tapped some keys, and the feed froze.

"Zoom in."

A couple more taps and the figure grew closer. Swift cleaned the image through some filters and soon all who stood there could see who it was. Cara shook her head.

"Fuck, I should have known there was only one crazy SOB dumb enough to jump out a window like that."

They were looking at Axe.

"Keep on him, Slick," Thurston snapped. "See if you can track him. And find out where that signal is coming from."

The general turned to Ferrero. "Inform Reaper of the new development. I just hope we can get to Axe before these assholes do."

———

CIA BLACK OPS BASE, WARSAW, POLAND

"Did you see that?" the computer tech said in disbelief. "He jumped out the fucking window."

"Yes, damn it," Newcomb snarled. "Get Greer after the bastard, now."

"Sir, there's a lot of radio traffic from the *Policja*. I count at least six units converging on their current location."

The CIA man nodded. "Noted."

"There is something else, too, sir."

Newcomb's patience had worn thin long ago, and now it was all but non-existent. "What?"

"I've picked up another signal. Whoever it is has piggybacked ours and can see what we see and hear our radio traffic."

"Christ!" Newcomb exploded. "It's got to be her."

"Who?"

"Thurston, dumbass! Order Greer out of there. We're packing up and moving. Tell him to keep looking. I'll send him a location when we're on the road."

"Yes, sir."

Newcomb turned to Nicole. "It looks like the game is afoot. This will no doubt be interesting. We're going to need more men now that Thurston and her team are here. Call Langley. Have Horn spinup Blackbird. I want them here within twelve hours."

Nicole nodded. Blackbird was a team of Delta operatives which the Special Activities Division used. They did what they were told, no questions asked. Greer's team were good. Bull Horton's Blackbird Team was the best.

———

MH-60K BLACK HAWK, SOMEWHERE OVER GERMANY

"We have a radio transmission for you, Gunny, from base," the Black Hawk captain's voice came through Kane's headset. I'll patch it through."

A heartbeat later, the same voice said, "You're on, Gunny."

"Go for Reaper One."

"Reaper One? Zero. We've had some new developments on our end. It seems our friends from back home have arrived, and they put the moves on Reaper Four."

Kane immediately grew anxious, not wanting to ask the obvious question. But he did. "Is he OK, Zero?"

"Apart from trying to fly from a second-floor window, he seems to be fine. He's currently in the wind."

"What about our friends?"

"We're trying to nail down a location. But if they've made us, then they'll disappear too. As for Reaper Four, we're trying to keep track of him until you arrive on station."

"Copy, Zero."

"Take care, Reaper. Zero out."

Kane glanced around the interior of the Black Hawk. He could just make out the others sitting across from him. To his left sat the crew chief. He leaned close and asked, "How much longer?"

"Twenty mikes."

Kane nodded. It might as well have been twenty days. He just hoped Axe was OK.

———

WARSAW, POLAND

Axe hurt. He was sure he had a cracked rib, if not two. There were a few cuts, one of them deep enough to need a stitch or six put in. He limped his way along the street and ducked into a dark alley. Straight away the smell of rotting garbage assailed his nostrils. He winced and kept limping. Although the pain in his right leg was subsiding, he assumed it would eventually stop. Not like the knife jabbing into his chest from his ribs.

He needed to find a place to lay up before his pursuers found him again. The trouble was he was going to need help. These guys had found him no problems. He needed to be better than they were, and in his condition, he was far from it.

Axe reached into his pocket for his burner cell and ran a number he knew from memory. He waited a few heartbeats until the person on the other end answered. "Yeah. It's me. I need your help."

CHAPTER 10

RAMSTEIN AIRFORCE BASE, GERMANY

THURSTON DIDN'T LOOK at the screen when she answered the cell. She just placed it to her ear and said, "Thurston."

"Yeah. It's me. I need your help."

"Axe?"

"Yes, ma'am."

A wave of relief washed over Thurston which was quickly replaced by anger. "Two questions, marine. Are you OK? And where the fuck are you? And what the hell were you thinking?"

"That's three, ma'am."

"Don't even go there, soldier," the general said as she waved at Ferrero to get his attention.

Axe said, "Yes, ma'am."

"Give me a sitrep, Axe. Leave nothing out."

Ferrero stopped in front of her, "You wanted, me, Mary?"

"I've got Axe, have Slick trace the call."

He hurried away, and Thurston went back to the call. "Sorry, keep going."

"No, ma'am, I'm sorry. I should never have come here."

"Don't worry about that now. Tell me what you need."

"They found me, ma'am. I'm pretty sure they're CIA."

"Yes, it's Newcomb with a team of killers. We saw what happened. Are you hurt? We saw you go out the window."

There was a pause at the other end, and for a moment, Thurston thought they'd been disconnected. "Axe?"

"I'm here, General. Sorry. I'm pretty sure I've got a couple of cracked ribs, I'm bleeding a bit, but my leg seems to be getting better. I need to locate a place to lay up for a while where they won't find me."

"I'll see what we can come up with. Keep moving and call me back in five minutes, Axe. OK? Reaper, Carlos, and Brick should be in Poland soon."

"Are you close, ma'am?"

"Closer than you think," she said and then hung up.

She looked across at Ferrero, "Were you able to get a location?"

Swift turned and said, "Somewhere in central Warsaw, ma'am."

"Good. Find me someplace he can lay up for at least twenty-four hours. Also, were you able to get anything on the vehicle those assholes were driving?"

"Make and model, ma'am, that's about it."

"It'll have to do. Get onto finding me a location. You've got four minutes," she glanced around and saw Cara and Reynolds staring at her. "Brooke, I want you to phone the *Policja* with the details of the vehicle those sons of bitches were driving. Do it anonymously. Check with Slick and then give them a ballpark location as to where they are."

"Copy, ma'am," the tall, athletically-built Reynolds snapped.

"General," Swift called out. "I think I might have something."

Thurston hurried over to where the computer tech was working. "What is it?"

"I've narrowed his signal down to this area here, ma'am," he said, pointing at the screen. He stabbed a finger at another point close to the flashing red dot and continued, "This building here is an old block of apartments slated for demolition. It's empty. Axe could hole up there."

"It's a death trap," Cara said. "If he gets caught in there he's done for."

"Not necessarily. At the top, there's a walkway across to the building next to it. He could get out there."

"Have the details ready for when he calls back," Thurston demanded.

"General, get me on a plane to Warsaw. If you do, I can be there long before Reaper and the others."

"No. I still have a job for you here."

Cara was about to argue the point when the cell in Thurston's pocket rang. She took it out and hit the accept button. "Yes?"

"It's me again, ma'am."

The general held out her hand for the piece of paper Swift had scribbled the details on. "Listen up, Axe. Three blocks to your east is an abandoned apartment block. You should be alright to hole up there until Kane and the others reach you sometime tomorrow. I want you to check in with me every hour, understood?"

"Yes, ma'am."

"What do you have in the way of firepower?"

"A handgun and an MP5 I took off one of the shooters."

"Good. Stay frosty, marine. Call me when you reach your objective."

———

WARSAW, POLAND

"Shit, we've got a problem, Hank."

Greer looked in the side mirror and saw the flashing lights of the Warsaw Police behind them. "Take it easy. Just pull over to the side."

The vehicle eased to the curb and stopped. Behind them, the police car did the same. Greer reached down and cleared his handgun. He took a suppressor from his pocket and screwed it on. He said, "Ease your seat back a touch, Grit."

The driver did as requested, and the men waited as two officers approached. "You ain't going to kill them, are you?" Grit asked his team leader.

"You want them to take us in?"

No answer.

"I didn't think so. Roll your window down. I'll do this side."

The two uniformed officers split up and walked along each side of the SUV. As soon as they reached the front windows, Greer reacted.

The officer opened his mouth to speak, only to have his words cut off by a bullet which flew into his maw and out the back in a spray of gore. The other officer was transfixed by what had happened to his partner, which gave Greer time to adjust his aim and shoot him too. One, two, just like that.

He started to unscrew the suppressor and said, "Drive."

———

WASHINGTON, D.C.

General Hank Jones was too old and set in his ways to change the habits of a lifetime, and that's what almost got him killed. Every day when he headed home from work, whether it be early afternoon or evening, he always had his driver stop at a small newspaper stand in Georgetown near the waterfront park. That afternoon was no different.

He had his driver pull over, and he exited the car. Walking perhaps thirty meters along a path which was lined with plants and trees, he then cut through the parklands. At a junction, he followed another path which cut back under Whitehurst Freeway and came to his destination.

"Early day, General?" the stand owner asked when he saw him.

"Date night with my wife, Marcus," Jones informed him.

Marcus smiled at him. "I thought you'd be too old for such foolishness, Hank?"

Jones chuckled. "I am, but Nancy still thinks we're young enough." He bent down and picked up a paper, turning back to look at the Potomac.

"Are you trying to see how far you'd get without paying before I ran your ass to the ground?"

He turned to look at his friend. Both men had served

in Vietnam together. Both had been officers. At the conclusion of the war, however, Marcus had chosen to get out, whereas Hank Jones had stayed in. Now one owned a newsstand, and the other was the chairman of the joint chiefs.

Jones dug into his pocket and took out a five dollar note. He passed it over to Marcus and just as he did, the newsman's head exploded.

The bullet was meant for him, of that he was sure. Witnessing the up-close death of his friend came as a huge shock, and Jones froze. Marcus dropped to the pavement and didn't move, a hole in his head just above the bridge of his nose.

Dumbly, Jones started to turn, but even as he did, another shot whacked into the newspaper stand, shredding a magazine.

"General! Get down!" a voice shouted. Jones turned and saw a man running toward him. He was a tall, thin man with short brown hair. He wore jeans and a shirt but in his hand was a SIG M-17 handgun. He shouted again. "General, get down!"

Another shot. This one snapped close to Jones' head and, as though someone had flicked a switch, he reacted. Dropping to the ground, he began to crawl for the cover of the stand. The man who'd shouted the warning now stood next to him, handgun raised. He snapped off two shots and leaned down to grasp Jones by his arm. "Let me help you, sir."

Then Jones heard his rescuer say, "Scimitar, this is Pop-Eye, we're taking fire, I say again, we're taking fire. Already have one civilian down."

The man helped get the general in behind the stand which offered scant cover. However, it obscured the line of sight of the shooter. Jones, still stunned, looked up and said, "Who are you, soldier?"

"Mike Oil, sir. SEAL Team..." Whack! "Shit! That was close."

"What's going on, here?"

"Well, sir, it would seem that some fellers are trying to kill you."

———

GEORGETOWN, WASHINGTON, D.C.

Chief Borden Hunt checked the loads in his handgun out of habit before exiting the dark-green SUV with Rucker and Pop-Eye. "Pop, you take the general. We'll take these other pricks and see what they're up to."

"Copy, boss," Pop-Eye said and started off through the park.

Hunt, callsign Scimitar was a Navy SEAL. They all were. What they were doing in Georgetown was shadowing Hank Jones as per the orders of their boss, Rear-Admiral Joe Alexander. *"Don't let him out of your damned sight,"* were his exact words.

Hunt was a man of average height and build, commanded his own team, and had helped Team Reaper of late on different missions. The last, a foray into Mexico and then into the Appalachian Mountains.

Today, however, was a covert mission. Over the past couple of days, all had been quiet. But this day, they had discovered they weren't the only ones following the general. Someone in a white van had latched onto his black town car once he'd left the Pentagon.

When the driver had pulled into the lot, they'd watched as Jones exited his car. Rucker, the team combat medic, said, "This is the third day in a row he's been here. He don't mix it up or anything."

"I think these guys know that too," Hunt said, indicating the four shooters who had just exited the van. All were armed with suppressed MP5s. "Get your comms in. This is a fucking hit."

Pop-eye moved to follow the general while Hunt and Rucker circled around to follow the shooters. Instead of sticking to the paths, they cut through the grassed areas. Hunt said into his comms, "Pop, you need to step it up a bit, or they'll get there before you."

"Copy, Chief."

"They're splitting up," Rucker observed.

Two of the shooters circled further left, and Hunt figured they were trying to come in from behind the newspaper stand. That way if the frontal attempt missed and spooked the general, he would attempt to escape in the opposite direction and run right into the second team. Typical hammer and anvil tactic.

Hunt said, "Ruck, take the first pair, I'll take the other two. Don't fuck it up. Put them down the first time."

"Copy that."

Hunt followed his pair as they made their way around to position themselves behind the newspaper stand. Suddenly his comms came to life. "Scimitar, this is Pop-Eye, we're taking fire, I say again, we're taking fire. Already have one civilian down."

"Copy, Pop. Hang on, we'll be there in a moment."

Hunt cursed under his breath and quickened his pace. He stopped behind a freeway support and watched as the shooters took up position and raised their weapons. Hunt stepped out, his M17 raised. "Hey, assholes."

They turned, surprised that someone was there to challenge them. Hunt squeezed his trigger twice, and both men dropped to the ground. Hurrying up to them, he placed two more shots into their heads. Looking around, he said into his comms, "Ruck, how are you doing?"

"I have two down and out of the fight, Chief."

"Copy. Mine are down and out too. Regroup on Pop's position."

"Roger that."

They gathered at the newspaper stand where they found Pop-Eye standing guard over Jones. Hunt took one look at him and asked, "Are you OK, General?"

"I will be. Who are you, and what are you doing here?"

"Chief Borden Hunt, sir. We were tasked to watch over you, sir."

"Hunt?" Jones asked thoughtfully.

"Yes, sir."

"Seems I should know that name."

"Scimitar, sir," Hunt said and then to Pop-Eye, "Lead out Pop. We have to get the general safe."

"Copy, Chief."

"Hold on a damned minute," Jones protested. "I'm not leaving Marcus like that."

"Sorry, sir, but we need you to get out of here. We killed four shooters, and I don't know if there are any more about. I am assuming that we got the guy that killed your friend."

Hunt was reasonably sure there weren't, but he needed to get Jones out of the open and back to safety. The general hesitated, and Hunt said, "Sir, once we get moving, I'll call it in and have someone come and take care of him."

Jones knew that was bullshit, but he didn't argue. He knew the chief was right. "What about my driver?"

"You can call him once we're on the road."

"All right, Chief. Lead out."

As they started to make their way through the park, sirens could be heard in the distance, growing louder with every step they took. The people who'd been in the park were now gone, scared away by the gunfire.

"Who tasked you, son?" Jones asked.

"Rear-Admiral Alexander, sir."

"He would."

RAMSTEIN AIRFORCE BASE, GERMANY

Thurston hung up the phone and stared at Ferrero. "Someone just tried to kill Hank Jones."

"Really?"

"Yes. In broad daylight. Georgetown Park. He was lucky. Joe Alexander had tasked Hunt and his men to watch his back. As it was, a friend of Hank's was killed."

Ferrero shook his head. "It would seem these people are more serious about stopping us than we first anticipated."

The general nodded.

"I bet he's pissed."

"Oh, yes. I could feel the heat from his breath coming through the phone."

"What are we to do, Mary?"

"He's green-lit us to hit these guys where it hurts," Thurston explained.

"The Mareks?" Ferrero asked.

She nodded. "Yes. First, we pick up Axe, and then we continue to find the son. We get him out alive."

"What about Gustaw?"

Thurston sighed. "We can't really go to war with the

Polish government, which is what we'd be doing if we went directly at him. But it doesn't mean we can't go after his business interests. First thing in the morning get Cara and Pete onto the interrogation of Falk. We'll find out what he knows. Between him and the son, we should be able to put a big dent in the older Marek's business ventures."

"And the CIA black ops team? They're going to keep coming at us."

"As long as they keep coming, we'll keep putting them down. No more fucking around, Luis. If these pricks want a war, then we'll give them just that. Get in touch with Reaper. Tell him that when it comes to the CIA team, he's weapons free."

"Yes, ma'am."

CHAPTER 11

GERMANY, NEAR THE POLISH BORDER

THE SOUND of the Black Hawk faded slowly into the distance, and the small team of three loaded their gear into the back of the black Range Rover. There was a silver moon overhead, and the light it threw lit the surrounding meadow with its dim glow. Kane was certain that if everything went right, they would be in Warsaw sometime before midday.

"Who's driving?" Brick asked.

"You are," Kane informed him.

"Cool. I won't complain."

"Just get us there in one piece, Amigo," Arenas said to him. "I was told that your driving was lacking in certain areas."

"Who told you that?"

"I would not like to say. I do not think the general would forgive me."

"That was one time," Brick snapped. "One damned time."

Arenas and Kane chuckled, and Brick knew he'd been taken for a ride.

"You bastards."

"All right, mount up. Let's get out of here."

They bumped across the field and found the road. Turning right, they were on their way and had gone about ten kilometers when the satellite phone rang. "Kane."

"Reaper, it's Luis. There's been some developments you need to be aware of."

"I'm listening."

Ferrero went on to tell him everything they knew about Axe and what had happened to Jones. He also advised him of Axe's present location. Once he was finished, Kane said, "I see a slight problem, Zero. All we have are handguns."

"I'm aware of that."

"But those guys are packing assault weapons."

"I'm aware of that too. If you have problems, take theirs."

"Copy," Kane said and hung up.

"What was that about?" Brick asked as he took a corner at speed.

Reaper looked at him and said, "We're fucked."

WASHINGTON, D.C.

The SUV eased to a stop with the sound of crunching gravel on the turnaround. Hunt and the others climbed out and waited for Jones to do the same. They escorted him toward the large house and up the steps to the massive oak front door. Somebody was up, the dim lighting which shone through one of the windows attesting to that.

Jones reached up and pressed the doorbell. After a few moments there was movement on the other side of the door, the sound of it being unlocked, and then it swung open to reveal a dark-haired man in a robe. The man glanced at the small group standing on his stoop and said, "Hank, what are you doing here?"

"I need to talk to you, Mr. Speaker. It's a matter of national security."

Speaker of the House Frank Clavell frowned. "Of course, Hank. Come in. What about your friends?"

"We're right here, sir," Hunt said.

Clavell nodded. "Fine. Come on in, Hank."

Jones stepped inside, and the door closed behind him.

———

Letting out an extra-long breath, Clavell tried to contemplate all that he'd just been told. He opened his mouth to speak, then closed it and thought some more.

"I know it's a lot to take in, Mr. Speaker. But I wouldn't be here if I thought there was another way."

The speaker of the house nodded. "I'm still trying to wrap my head around the fact that someone had the balls to try and kill you in broad daylight. But to think that the vice-president is somehow involved with it too, that's a whole other thing altogether."

"It is. However, they're all connected. I'm only assuming that Black Shield are responsible for the hit. Or it could have come from Paul Horn at the CIA Special Activities Division. But the order to hand everything over-came directly from Jim Forth. They were making sure that the video we have doesn't get out. I know that Black

Shield stand to lose billions if the deal with the Poles falls through and that they're one of the biggest campaign contributors for the president. But I can't imagine him being behind this. Maybe he doesn't even know."

Clavell hesitated before saying, "I'm going to tell you something, and it doesn't leave this room, Hank. Understand? If it gets out, there'll be trouble for not just you."

"Yes, sir."

"There is a chance that the president may not run for another term. I'm not sure yet, and I can't go into details. But if he doesn't, then Jim Forth will more than likely run."

Jones stared at him for a moment and then said, "If that's true, sir, then it gives Jim Forth a real reason for this not to get out."

"Maybe. But why have you come to me with this?"

"You hear things, sir. You can find things out. I can't do this on my own. I'm not political enough."

Clavell thought for a while about what Jones was asking him to do. "What about your team in Europe, Hank?"

"They're in good hands with Mary. They'll do their job no matter what gets thrown at them. They've proved that many times."

"I don't want them declaring open war on each other in a foreign country. Understood?"

"They'll just do their job, sir. However, if they're attacked, they won't back away from it. Sir, can I be open with you?"

"Sure, Hank."

"Sir, the World-Wide Drug Initiative as it's known, was formed to take the war on drugs to all corners of the globe. One part of that globe is Poland. Gustaw Marek is a big producer of Ecstasy in Europe. I've instructed the team to make a dent in his production while leaving him alone. His son, on the other hand, is directly responsible for the death of an American. They will pick him up and question him about it. And if necessary, they'll get him out of the country and bring him back here to face charges for his crime."

"That's walking a fine line, Hank."

"Yes, sir."

"All right, Hank, I'll help any way I can. Give me a couple of days, and I'll see what I can come up with. Do you want a special detail?"

"No, sir, Joe Alexander's boys will do. They're good, and I trust them."

"Fine, fine. I'll give you a call when I have something."

"Thank you, sir."

BLACK SHIELD INDUSTRIES, WASHINGTON, D.C.

The cell rang, and Drake answered it. The caller on the other end was Paul Horn. "The hit failed."

Drake leaned forward in his chair, a look of frustration on his face. "How?"

"It wasn't anticipated that Jones had some guys watching him. They killed the team that was sent after him. My man has gone to the ground."

"Then send someone else, damn it."

"No. We took our chance, and it fucked up. You'll have to do it from the inside."

"How?"

"Tell Forth to shut them down."

"He can't. The president is the only one who can do that. He already told them to back off and hand everything over. If he tries to shut them down, it'll start a shit storm."

"Well, I guess that only leaves us one avenue."

"That is?" asked Drake.

"We take them all out. You'll need to prep a team to send to Ramstein, Germany."

"What?"

"That's where they are."

"How do you know this?"

"I work for the CIA. I know everything."

"And how am I meant to get at them there?" Drake asked.

"That's your problem," Horn told him and hung up. Things were getting way too out of hand.

———

RAMSTEIN AIRFORCE BASE, GERMANY

The Humvee pulled up outside the hangar at eight the next morning, and two Air Commandos climbed out followed by Fabian Falk, Europe's biggest drug manufacturer. He was dressed in a green jumpsuit and had leg chains as well as those on his wrists. With a jingle at every step, he was escorted inside, and the commandos led him to a table where they sat him in a seat. They then took a few steps back and waited, standing guard.

Cara and Pete Traynor had watched him shuffle in. The drug manufacturer was somewhere in his early forties, had a beard, and they figured him to be just over six-feet tall.

"So that's the most wanted drug manufacturer in Europe, huh?" Cara said.

Traynor nodded. "Yeah. The guy has been like grease,

slipped through every net Interpol and every other law enforcement agency threw up. I've seen pictures of him, but with the stories that surround this guy, you'd think he was ten-feet tall."

Pete Traynor was an ex-DEA agent who'd spent a lot of time undercover in Mexico at one time or another. He'd come across to Team Reaper when it was first banded together. Him, Ferrero, Kane, and Cara were the initial members. He was a tall man in his late thirties, unshaven, tattooed arms, with brown eyes and broad shoulders.

"How do you want to do this?" Cara asked.

"You're the ex-cop, how about you lead?"

"The big-bad DEA agent want to see how it's done?"

Traynor smiled. "Oh, yeah. I want to see how you crack his nuts."

Thurston approached them. "Remember, we need him to talk. Anything he knows about Marek especially."

"You want us to use that angle, ma'am?" Cara asked.

"Yes," she passed Cara a folder.

Cara opened it, flicked through and then closed it back up. "All right then, let's see what we can come up with."

Crossing to the table, they pulled out their chairs. Only Cara sat down, Traynor put his hands on the back of his and stood there like some overbearing father figure. Thurston was in the background, letting her people run with it. Fabian Falk looked first at Cara and then Traynor, then went back to fiddling disinterestedly with the links of his chains.

Cara stared hard at him. "I'm Smith, he's Jones," she said, drawing on the television series from her childhood, Alias Smith and Jones, which had run in untold amounts of repeats. "We'll be your friends today. Anything you need, just ask."

Traynor cleared his throat. "How come I get to be Jones. Why can't I be Smith? I think I look like a Smith." He glanced at Falk. "Don't you think I look like a Smith?"

Falk glanced at him.

Cara sighed. "Fine, you be Smith."

"Nope, don't want to now."

"OK, be Jones."

"Thought I already was?"

Focusing on Falk, she could see he was watching their banter go back and forth. Good, they had him interested.

"You know, Fabian," Cara said, using his first name, "I thought you'd be bigger. Like your reputation. But you're no taller than me. I must say, I'm disappointed."

He shrugged.

Interaction, another plus.

"Have you eaten this morning? Had something to drink?"

"Is this how it is to be?" he asked in heavily-accented English. "Soften me up so I will talk to you?"

Traynor stared hard at him. "No. You will talk. How it happens is up to you."

Falk glared at the ex-DEA man. "Fuck you, asshole." Traynor feigned being wounded by the insult.

"What can you tell me about, Gustaw Marek?" Cara asked.

Shifting his gaze, Falk said, "Nothing."

"Come on, Fabian. You're the most hired manufacturer of drugs in Europe. Everyone wants your services. You can't tell us you haven't worked for him before."

"I've worked for many people."

"We're not interested in other people," Traynor said. "Just Marek."

"Who?"

Cara said, "If you're scared of him, we can help you."

"I doubt it."

So, he was scared. The folder Thurston had given Cara sat in front of her. She opened it and on top was a blank piece of paper. "What do you think I have in here, Fabian?"

He looked at it and shrugged.

"Would you like to see?"

Again, he shrugged.

Cara took the piece of paper away and revealed the picture of a woman, early thirties, long black hair, maybe Italian. She placed it on the table in front of Falk. When she did, it revealed another picture, this one of a girl perhaps ten, almost the image of her mother.

She repeated her actions, and the face of a boy appeared. A little younger than the girl, but again, the same facial features as his mother.

Falk moved uncomfortably in his seat. Cara said, "Nice family. Are they still in Italy? Tuscany? Lovely part of the world. Sienna, I believe."

Falk became defensive again. "Fuck you," he hissed.

"If I had a family like that, I'd be scared too. Marek must be a hard man, yes? Has to be to have gotten where he is. Does he have his own personal hitmen? Who'll protect them after you're shipped back to the U.S.?"

Falk said nothing.

"It won't really matter for you, though. Once you're Stateside, you'll never have contact with them again. So, you won't know if they're alive or dead, will you?"

Staring into space, Falk remained silent, however, the set of his jaw told Cara all she needed to know. Even though he was a criminal, he was still a family man. "What will it take for you to talk to us, Fabian?"

He glanced up at her, his mind working as he processed what she'd just said. Opening his mouth briefly, he paused before anything came out, then snapped it shut.

"Do you have something to say?" Traynor asked in a less confronting tone.

"Do you want us to take care of your family, Fabian?" Cara asked him. "Is that it?"

She could see it was. Turning in her seat, she shot a questioning glance back at Thurston. The general nodded her approval and Cara turned back. "What if we can arrange for your family to be transported back to the U.S? Keep them safe, put them in a new house, take care of them? Will that do?"

"No. I want to be with them."

"Not going to happen. You have a date with a nice cold cell."

"Then I have nothing to say," he growled.

Cara thought for a moment then motioned to Traynor. He leaned in close, and Cara whispered into his ear, "What if we can get them into witness protection Stateside, and the DEA can use him as an informant for drug operations in Europe?"

"It might work. We'd need to get clearance first."

Nodding, Cara came to her feet, and they both left the table, walking across to Thurston's observation point. "What is it?"

"Ma'am, we figure that if we can get Falk and his family back home, the DEA can set them up somewhere under the proviso that he spills about the European drug trade. He'd be a high-value informant and source for them. If we can offer that, there might be a greater chance that he will give us what we need on Marek."

Thurston looked at Traynor. "What do you think?"

"I think it's sound, ma'am. He's like a vault waiting to be opened. All we need is the key."

"All right. I'll make a call. But I want something in return."

"Copy."

They returned to the table. This time they both sat down. Cara said, "Our boss is making a call, but she wants something in good faith. Something we can check, so we know that you're on the level."

"Call about what?"

"About you and your family."

"I will talk then. Not before."

"No, you give us something now, or I'll tell her not to bother," Cara snapped. Her voice grew hard, "Don't fuck with me, Fabian, or it'll all go away. You are this close to making a deal of a lifetime, and you are going to blow it, for what?"

He stared into her eyes and then said, "How about the location of his biggest ecstasy lab?"

"In Poland?"

"No, Latvia."

———

CIA SAFEHOUSE, WARSAW, POLAND

"Sir, I think we might have something," the computer tech said to Newcomb as he walked past.

The black ops team was set up in a double-story CIA safehouse in southern Warsaw. It was a large building on a small estate of about two acres. The house itself was set back off the road with well-tended gardens, a high-security fence, and security cameras all around. Also, there were motion sensors scattered throughout the grounds.

Inside was new, clean, modern. The team was set up in the large dining room; their equipment spread out across every available surface. Since their arrival, the team's computer guy had been working hard to find Axe. Now, it would seem, his tenacity had paid off.

Nicole joined Newcomb at the tech's side, the CIA man asking, "What is it?"

"I tried tracking our target using street cameras, security, stuff like that but I eventually lost him. However, I was able to get into the NSA servers and get some satellite footage from one of their birds. It would seem that one of those tasked to fly over Russia also happens to pass over Warsaw. And somehow, by pure dumb luck, it managed to pick up this."

He hit a key and brought up a picture on his laptop. It showed Axe walking along a narrow street.

The tech continued. "With this new information, I managed to find a string of cameras which led me to here."

Another picture flashed up of a block of rundown apartments. "He's in there."

"Are you sure?"

"Yes, sir. My guess is that he's laying up waiting for someone."

Newcomb glanced at Nicole. "The rest of the team? I thought we had them tracked to Ramstein?"

"As far as I know, they're still there," Nicole said. "Unless they've a team inbound to pick him up for extraction."

Newcomb nodded. "I think you're right. Get Greer and the rest of his team over there now. Have them sit on the place until the others show. And tell him to wait until they're inside and then breach. Kill them all."

"Yes, sir."

CHAPTER 12

WARSAW, POLAND

"PULL UP HERE," Kane told Brick. "That's the place across the road."

The SUV came to a halt alongside the curb, and the three men looked up at the five-floor, rundown apartment block on the opposite side of the street. It was an old concrete construction with most of the windows smashed. Some of the balconies retained ownership of piles of junk left by long-gone tenants. Graffiti adorned the external walls of the bottom floor, the perfect height within easy reach for artists with spray cans. A temporary mesh construction fence enclosed both that building and the one adjacent, a sign in Polish attached to it, informing any interested parties of what the future held for the land currently occupied by the blocks of derelict apartments.

In the back, Arenas looked around the street. Apart from a couple of cars and one pedestrian walking in the opposite direction, it looked reasonably quiet. The sidewalks were a little overgrown with grass, and there was plenty of rubbish lying in the gutters.

"I think we're clear," he said.

Kane said, "All right, comms in."

He punched in a number for the satellite phone, and Thurston answered. "Ma'am, we're on site and about to enter the building."

"Listen, Reaper, I've tried to contact Axe, but I can't get through. His cell has probably gone flat but just in case, be careful."

"Any more on Newcomb?"

"Negative. They went dark, and we lost them. We don't have visual, Reaper. You're on your own for this one. Once you get Axe, find a place to lay up, somewhere very public like a hotel. Then call me back for further orders."

"Copy, ma'am."

"Good luck."

Thurston hung up, and Kane tucked the phone in his pocket. He put his comms in and said to the others, "Take everything you need. Brick, bring the medic pack. The general hasn't been able to raise Axe so be alert. It may just be a dead cell, or it could be worse. Right, let's go."

Alighting from the SUV, they glanced around once more before starting across the street. Their M17s were tucked into their belts, out of sight. Gaining access through a gap in the mesh fence, they climbed through silently and moved to the front door and tried it. With a click, it opened, and after drawing their weapons, they slipped inside.

————

"Right, they've gone inside," Greer said to his team. "We follow and take them down. You've seen the blueprints. Rick, Chuck, you take stairwell two. Like we planned. With Kent and me taking one there'll be no way down. Sims, you stand sentry on the entrance just in case someone does slip past. If anything, they'll likely go up. Good for us, bad for them. Any questions?"

No one said a word. They were all clear on what was required of them.

"OK. Let's do this," Greer said. Then into his comms, "Raven Base? Raven One, we're breaching now, over."

"Copy, Raven One. Raven Base out."

The stench of stale urine was the first thing to assail the nostrils of Reaper and the others as they pushed in through the door. Someone had obviously come off the street and taken a piss in there. They wrinkled their noses then brushed it aside.

Starting up the stairs to the first floor, they reached the landing and stopped. Reaper said, "We're going to have to clear these floors one at a time until we find him."

Arenas stood watching in the hallway as Kane and Brick made their way methodically down the corridor to the end. The first door opened, producing the rancid smell of mold and other unknown matters. Overall, the once white walls were covered in graffiti, the drywall contained more holes than Swiss cheese, and most of the doors to the apartments were open, some off their hinges.

Reaper swept the first bedroom in the initial apartment. It contained a stinking mattress, covered in stains. The wall had multiple tags of some descript, most painted around the many holes.

He came out and entered the filthy kitchen-come-living room. Brick had already cleared it and proceeded into the second bedroom. It too still held a steel-framed bed. The mattress slashed and burgeoning its ancient horse-hair stuffing. That left the bathroom for Kane to clear. Again, empty.

They met back in the living room. "This is going to take forever if we have to do this, Reaper," Brick said.

Kane nodded. "It's the only way, other than telegraph our presence. And if Newcomb and his goons are around, then we'll be in trouble."

They managed to clear the remaining three apartments reasonably efficiently before reaching the other end and the door to the second stairwell. Arenas opened it and immediately pulled back. "There is someone coming up the stairs."

Kane slipped his head out the door and peered down the stairwell. There were two men armed with suppressed MP5s. He eased back through the door and closed it. "Back. Get back; it's Newcomb's men."

They hurried back along the hallway and were outside the third apartment when the door at the other end made a noise and began to open.

"Fuck!" Reaper cursed softly. "In there."

They moved into the third apartment and eased the door closed just as Greer appeared, sweeping the hallway with his weapon.

"I guess we're kind of trapped, huh?" Brick said.

Kane's eyes darted around the room and focused on the sliding glass door which led out onto the balcony. Hurrying across to it, he tried the door. It rattled and bumped as it slid along its dirty and damaged track. Arenas and Brick stared at him, and the latter said, "Don't tell me he's looking to jump off another building."

Arenas gave him a grim smile. "I didn't see a pool down there, my friend, did you?"

"Shit."

Kane looked over the edge of the rail to the ground some fifteen feet below, and the first thing he saw was the man standing guard. Stepping back, he thought some more. Staying put meant that before too long, Newcomb's men would find them. And the bastards were equipped with automatic weapons. Sure, they could make a fight of it, but eventually they would take casualties and possibly all wind up dead.

He stepped forward again, taking another furtive look down. The man was no longer there but couldn't have gone far; he'd been put there for a reason. That ruled out that direction. Then he looked up.

"You ain't thinking what I think you are, are you Reaper?"

Kane looked at him. "We can't stay here."

Brick shook his head. "I knew it was a bad idea coming to work for you."

"Could be worse," Kane said, tucking his M17 into his belt. "We could be higher. Carlos, keep an eye on the ground. They've posted a sentry. If he looks up, pop him."

Arenas moved to the balcony rail and peered down, his handgun up in a firing position. "Whenever you are ready, amigo."

Kane climbed up onto the rail and reached overhead to get a grip on the edge of the floor of the balcony above. The rail wobbled perilously, and for a moment, it looked as though it might collapse under his weight. He just hoped the one above was in better shape than this one.

Reaper steadied himself, sucked in a deep breath, and pulled himself up. His legs flailed about in mid-air as his right hand shot up to grab the bottom part of the rail above. It held. Then he swung a leg up, using his mighty core strength to hook it on the edge of the balcony.

Pulling himself up, he eased over it and onto the filthy floor surface. He turned and looked back down. There was still no sign of the sentry. He signaled to Brick, and the ex-SEAL climbed up onto the rail.

Gritting his teeth, he copied the moves he'd watched Kane perform. Once within reach, Kane grasped his arm and started to haul him over the rail. But things weren't meant to go smoothly for the team, and when Kane had Brick almost over the rail, it collapsed, and the ex-SEAL was stranded hanging in midair.

Most of the rail hit the external pavement with a loud rattle. Below, the sentry appeared and looked up.

"Hijo de puta!" Arenas swore and fired down at the man. BLAM! BLAM!

The operator rocked back and fell to the ground. Both rounds had penetrated on a downward trajectory behind the man's vest, ripping through muscle and vital organs. He coughed blood and went still.

While this was happening, Kane gritted his teeth and dragged Brick over the edge of the balcony.

"Carlos, move!" Kane shouted. "Hurry, before they get here."

Too late, the door crashed back, and an operator filled the void, his MP5 raised to fire. Arenas beat him to the punch, firing a handful of shots that peppered all around the shooter, none hitting, but they had the desired effect. He disappeared out into the hallway. Arenas blew off three more rounds and then stuffed the M17 into his belt. Then, without hesitation, he leaped at the hands reaching down to haul him up.

It was like riding an invisible elevator. Kane and Brick's combined strength lifted him easily to the next level. Arenas gained his feet, and he said, "I do not like Poland."

Brick smiled. "I actually think it's starting to grow on me."

"Come on, let's get out of here before they trap us on this floor."

Hurrying through the apartment and out into the hall, they'd almost made it to the second stairwell when a familiar face appeared from the last doorway. "About time you showed up. I was getting lonely around here."

Kane was so wired he almost shot him. The M17 came up, and his finger flexed on the trigger. He was only a hair away from putting a bullet in his friend's face. "What the fuck, Axe?"

The big man limped out into the hallway. "What's all the shooting?"

"Newcomb's team has found us."

"Shit. What now?"

Kane reached out and relieved him of the MP5. He checked the magazine and said, "We're getting the hell out of here. Brick, rear security. Carlos on me, Axe, you take number three."

Of course, they picked the wrong stairwell. The law of averages gave them a fifty percent chance of being right. But there was always the other fifty percent. The one they chose.

As soon as Reaper hit the stairwell, he heard them coming up. He reversed and thought for a moment. "All right. Back up."

They did so by moving toward the far stairwell. At the halfway point along the hallway, Kane directed them into an apartment. Once inside, Kane said, "We wait until they're in the hallway and then we take them. I'll go first and then Carlos you leapfrog me and then Brick you do the same. We'll bring down a suppressing fire, and hopefully, we'll take them by surprise."

"Roger that."

"Roger that."

"I'm just going to burn through this first mag on the MP5 so be ready to move. It's all about suppression."

The hinges on the door at the end of the hallway squeaked as it swung open. Kane waited, counted to twenty, then moved. He stepped out into the middle of the hallway, the MP5 up in the firing position.

There were four operators making their way along the hallway. All wore tactical vests and carried MP5s. Reaper's sudden appearance took them by surprise. So much so, that they hesitated.

Kane let rip with a sustained burst from his weapon. It burned through the magazine in a heartbeat. He dropped to his knee and clawed at his M17. Behind him, Arenas was already moving. His handgun up as he methodically squeezed the trigger.

The first man in the line was already falling when Arenas emerged. Three rounds from Kane's MP5 had done their bloody work. One had hit the vest, while two others had torn open the man's throat. The wounds sprayed their own graffiti on the painted walls.

Arenas concentrated on the second operator. Of the first four shots, three hit him in the chest, punching him back into the man behind him. Unable to free up a weapon, this third shooter was an easy target for the ex-Mexican special forces commander as he placed two rounds in his head.

Once Arenas was dry, Brick emerged and leapfrogged them both. He shot the struggling man that Arenas had stopped dead with the rounds to the chest. Then he shifted aim to the last shooter, the bald man with the beard who was retreating and firing at the same time.

Slugs ripped into the walls and ceiling as the man fired wildly trying to stop the advancing figure. Brick felt the heat of a passing round and fired twice more, one of the bullets clipping the man's left shoulder, eliciting a cry of pain. He reeled away and disappeared out the doorway and down into the stairwell.

"Moving!" Brick snapped, and the team combat medic pressed further forward, weapon still raised to cover the opening.

Behind him, Kane and Arenas came to their feet. They trailed the man in front as he moved to clear ahead. Brick stepped over the fallen black ops operators and continued. He'd just reached the doorway when Greer suddenly appeared.

The MP5 in his hands was a millisecond away from firing when Brick moved, his left hand sweeping the lethal weapon away just in time. Greer's finger depressed the trigger and, the bullets which blasted from the MP5's muzzle hammered into the wall.

Brick took another half a step forward, bringing his head down in a savage blow. His forehead hit the bridge of Greer's nose and shattered it. With a howl of pain, the operator's head snapped back. Brick brought his M17 up and rammed the barrel under the killer's chin and pulled the trigger.

The slug exploded upward through Greer's mouth and into his brain, eventually exiting from the top of his bald head with a sickening wet sound. He dropped at Brick's feet in a bloody heap and didn't move. "We're clear."

They checked the bodies to ensure there would be no surprises and then riffled the pockets for anything of value. They were clean except for their comms and a set of keys to a vehicle.

"Time to get out of here before the police show up. Axe, are you good?"

"I'm good, Reaper. But where are we going?"

"Back to Ramstein."

"But..."

"No buts, get your ass moving. I've a feeling that Thurston is going to tear a chunk out of it when we get there."

———

CIA SAFEHOUSE, WARSAW, POLAND

"Sir, Raven Team is down, including Raven One."

"Fuck!" Newcomb swore vehemently. "What the hell happened?"

"I don't know, sir."

He glared at Nicole. She shrugged her shoulders. "Don't look at me."

"How far away is Blackbird?"

"They should be here sometime this evening."

"When they arrive, bring them up to speed. This whole situation is getting out of fucking control."

CHAPTER 13

RAMSTEIN AIRFORCE BASE, GERMANY

CARA SLAPPED the sheet of paper on the table and sat down next to Traynor. She turned it around and pushed it across so Falk could see it. "This is your deal, Falk. Read it, and then start talking."

The drug manufacturer read through it and nodded. "OK."

"Just so you still understand, you fuck with us, it's gone, and you spend the rest of your life being some-body's bitch in a supermax somewhere."

"I understand. Where do you want to start?"

Cara depressed the red record button on the device she'd brought with her.

Traynor said, "Let's start with something easy. How many labs does he have?"

"Three. He has one in Slovakia, the one in Latvia, and the third is in Ukraine. He launders his money through Belarus."

"How does he ship his product?" Cara asked.

"He uses trucks. Pays off the right people, and they are left alone. Everything goes out through Gdańsk on the Baltic Coast."

"And who would suspect a prominent man in the Polish government?" Cara said sarcastically.

Traynor leaned forward on his elbows. "What about security?"

"Jednostka Wojskowa Komandosów."

Cara raised her eyebrows. "Polish Special Forces?"

"Ex-special forces. He pays good money. More than what the army pays."

"How many at each site?"

Falk wiggled his head from side to side. "It varies. Most of the time it is maybe fifteen. Latvia, because it is his biggest, would have twenty."

Swift approached the table where they sat, a folder in his hand. He passed it to Cara. "I think this is it."

Inside the folder were satellite photos of what was supposed to be Marek's Latvian operation. She pushed it across the table in front of Falk and asked him, "Is this it? The Latvian lab?"

Falk studied the picture. It wasn't actually one factory, but a complex of disused buildings, warehouses. There were four larger ones in total, rundown, junk scattered about on the surrounding concrete apron. The exterior of it all was encompassed by a large pine forest. Falk nodded. "That is it."

"It looks like a disused dump," Traynor observed.

"Yes, deliberately left that way. Inside it is different."

"How far from the nearest town?"

"An hour. The site was chosen well. It is surrounded by the forest, and perhaps one-thousand meters out on all sides is a large perimeter fence. The *Fricis* River runs along the back boundary of the complex."

Cara's eyes ran over the buildings. She reached into her pocket and took out a pen. Passing it across to Falk, she said, "In case you get a notion to stab someone with that, understand that one of us will shoot you in the head if you try. Now, take it and mark the factory building."

Falk stared at her as though he'd been contemplating doing just that, and she'd read his mind, then he made an X on the photo. Surprisingly it wasn't the biggest of the warehouses. "It is that one."

"You're sure?"

"Yes." He made another X on the photo. This time it was the biggest one. "He keeps all of his chemicals in here. And this one," another X, "is where the guards and workers sleep."

"Where do the workers come from?"

"Slaves. Poor people who need the money. The thing is, once they work in the labs, there is no going back. They are told the money will be sent back to their families. Marek keeps it for himself. They are poorly fed, and once they're past their best, they are killed."

"Asshole," Traynor growled. "How does he stay under the radar?"

"Money buys a lot of silence. But when that doesn't work, bullets will do," Falk explained. "Do you remember two years ago when the Polish foreign minister's car blew up with him inside it?"

Cara nodded. "Yes. It was blamed on ISIS."

"Only because everything else was blamed on ISIS too. It was a phase. Most of the blame was well placed. Except for this. When have you known ISIS to go after just one person?"

"You're saying it was Marek who was responsible for it?"

"Yes."

Cara glanced at Traynor, and then her gaze drifted back to Falk. "All right. That'll do for today. We'll talk some more tomorrow."

She waved at the air commandos, and they came across and secured Falk. He looked at Cara. "What about my family?"

"They're being picked up as we speak. Take him away; we'll continue tomorrow."

Once Falk was taken away, Ferrero came over to the pair. "How did it go?"

"Good," Traynor replied. "We'll have another run at him tomorrow. But what he's told us so far seems to hold water."

Cara held out the recorder. "You and the general might want to listen to it. There's some good stuff on there, especially the part about Marek blowing up a government minister."

"Really?"

"Uh, huh. And the strange thing is, I actually believe him."

"Me too," Traynor said.

"Fair enough. Just so you know, Kane and the others are on their way back with their package."

"Are they OK?"

"As far as I know. We won't find out any more until they get back this evening. I'll take this recording to Mary. Good job so far."

————

The MH-60K Black Hawk touched down as the setting sun started to disappear below the horizon, leaving a red glow in its wake. The four-team members disembarked with their gear. As Cara watched them walk across the pavement, a feeling of relief that they had returned safely washed over her. As soon as they were close enough, she stepped forward and wrapped her arms around Axe. "You stupid big ox. What were you thinking?"

"Apparently I wasn't."

"We're all sorry about your sister, Axe. But you can't go running off like that. You almost got yourself killed."

"Not my finest moment, Billings. Not at all. How's the boss?"

"I guess you'll find out when we get back to the hangar."

Axe winced. "Maybe I should just shoot myself in the foot and get sent home now."

"Come on, big feller," Kane said, slapping him on the shoulder. "Time to face the music."

Axe flinched. "Easy, Reaper. Jumped out a window, remember?"

———

"How is he?" Thurston asked Kane before she made a final decision on what to do with Axe.

"A few cuts and scrapes. Brick had to put a few stitches in his hide, but nothing too serious."

She nodded. "I'm going to send your team out in the next few days. But I need more information on the area of operation before you go."

"Where, ma'am?"

"Latvia. I'll fill you in tomorrow. Just so you know, Axe will be benched for this op."

Kane nodded. "I understand, General. He's not in any shape to go anyway."

"Get some rest. Tomorrow after we get the rest of the

information from Falk, you and the others can prep for your mission."

"Yes, ma'am."

Kane left, and Thurston made a gesture for Axe to join her. He looked almost sheepish standing there waiting for her to speak. "Come with me."

He followed Thurston out of the hangar and around the corner of the building. She stopped and turned to face him. "How are you feeling?"

"OK, I guess, ma'am."

She stared at him in the slowly diminishing light. Silent. Brooding. Then her face changed as her anger got the better of her. "What the fuck did you think you were doing? You not only put yourself at risk but the lives of your friends as well."

"I'm sorry, ma'am."

"Damn right you're fucking sorry. I know how you feel about your sister, Axe. We all felt your loss. But there's a right way and a wrong way of getting things done. And you just royally fucked up. You're lucky I don't have your ass on a C-17 Stateside right now. I damned well thought about it, believe me. Doing dumb shit like that on your own. And you couldn't even wait for Remy's service?"

Her last words stung. They were meant to. He winced and opened his mouth to speak. "I wasn't thinking, ma'am."

"Not about your sister you weren't."

He nodded. "I guess I'll take that C-17 now."

"The hell you will. You're here for the duration. The team is going on an op in the next few days. However, you'll stay on base. You're benched. Got it?"

He knew there would be no use arguing with her. "Got it, ma'am."

"All right. Dismissed."

He began to turn away, but Thurston stopped him. "Axe?"

"Yes, General?"

"I'm glad you're back in one piece."

"Thank you, ma'am."

———

WARSAW-MODLIN AIRPORT, POLAND

Externally, the Boeing 737 looked just like a normal passenger plane, but it was far from that. As it disgorged its twelve passengers dressed totally in black, one could understand why. They tromped down the stairs pushed up to the aircraft's door. Each carried a rucksack with any gear they had needed for the long flight. The rest of their stuff was in the cargo hold.

Bull Horton tasked his men with various things which needed to be accomplished before they left the airport. Then he turned to face the smiling man who'd been expecting him. Mark Newcomb offered him his hand, and Horton took it.

Horton was six-five tall, solid, had the customary beard, and deep-set blue eyes. When he spoke, his voice reminded one of Darth Vader from Star Wars. "Good to see you, Mark. What can we do for you?"

"It's a sensitive one this, Bull. A case of national security. You'll be going against some of our own. Are we going to have a problem with that?"

"You're sending me against CIA?"

Newcomb shook his head. "No. Have you ever heard of a team called Reaper?"

Bull shook his head. "Nope. Can't say I have. Met a

recon-marine one time who they called Reaper. Ice-cool motherfucker."

"Sounds like our man," Newcomb said.

Bull Horton raised his eyebrows. "If we're going after him, then this must be serious. He's not a man to be taken lightly."

"Don't I know it. They took out Hank Greer's Raven Team."

Bull gave a low whistle. "That's no mean feat."

"They made it look easy."

"Well then, you'd best point us in the right direction and turn us loose."

"That I will, Bull. Just as soon as I work out where they are."

———

THE PENTAGON, WASHINGTON, D.C.

The phone on Hank Jones' desk rang, and he picked it up after the third ring. "Jones."

"Hank, Frank Clavell. Have you got a moment?"

"Yes, sir."

"I've been digging around, and it would seem that our vice-president has been working behind the scenes to shore up support to have a crack at the big man's job. He's been collecting donors for a sizeable war chest. The biggest of which is Black Shield. It seems that you are right, Hank. It looks like there's been a deal done between Black Shield and Jim Forth. I'd say that in return for a sizeable donation, Forth has guaranteed Ken Drake the contract for the missile defense system."

"But doesn't that depend on Marek in Poland?"

"I'd say that there's a good chance Drake is greasing the wheels on that end as well."

"But what if the president decides to stay on?"

"It won't much matter. Forth has been driving this from the beginning."

"So, what can we do?"

"I don't know yet. Sit tight. When I do, then I'll let you know."

"Yes, sir."

The phone went dead, and Jones stared at the figure of Hunt sitting in the chair opposite. "Sit tight, my fucking ass. Chief, it's time to fight back. How are your abduction skills?"

LANGLEY, VIRGINIA

Paul Horn wasn't a man who was easily flustered. But things were starting to turn bad in one hell of a hurry, and he didn't like it. In fact, he despised failure, and that was all that he seemed to be getting of late.

Thurston and her people knew about their operation in the desert, they'd killed one of his black ops teams, Jones has escaped the assassination attempt, and there was the incident in Los Angeles.

But hopefully, with Bull Horton and his Blackbird team in Europe, things might just turn around. The last thing any of the conspirators could afford was for Gustaw Marek to pull out of their deal. A lot of money had been spent to get this far, but if Marek withdrew, everything would be lost. Hence the need to silence the Pakistani. If proof got out about the drone strike gone wrong, the voters would leave in droves, and Forth would never get back into the Whitehouse. And then there was no guarantee that the new administration would select Black Shield for the contract. He just hoped that Drake didn't fuck up his part in dealing with Thurston in Germany.

The phone on his desk rang, and he picked up the receiver. "Horn."

"I hope you're not too busy, Paul," the voice said.

"Not for you, Mr. Speaker."

"Good. I wanted to discuss something with you. It has come to my attention that you have an operation running in Europe."

"We have several of those, sir."

"I'm sure you know the one I mean, Paul," Clavell said. "Would you like me to spell it out for you so that we're clear?"

"Always the best way."

"Team Reaper."

"I see."

"Call your people back home, Paul. Before it gets out of hand."

It's already out of fucking hand. "I can't do that, sir."

"Can't or won't?"

"Sir, it is a matter of national security. They are all implicated in the theft of sensitive material."

"What material, Paul?"

"I can't say, sir."

"Like I said. Bring your damned team home, Paul, before it gets out of hand."

The line went dead.

"Fuck you, sir."

———

WASHINGTON, D.C.

Vice-President Jim Forth sat behind his desk with his dark-haired secretary astride his thighs. Her blouse was open, and his face was buried between her medium-sized breasts. She giggled and bounced around, eliciting a low growl.

Forth drew his head back and looked up at her, a broad grin on his face. Between his exposed teeth was a strawberry. He spoke around it his voice muffled, "Got it."

His secretary touched his nose with her finger and said, "I knew you could, Jimmy. You are just so skilled at doing things with that mouth of yours."

He sucked the piece of fruit into his mouth and started to chew it vigorously. "Shall we try something else?"

"Oh, yes."

The phone rang. "Shit." He answered it. "What?"

"We have a problem."

Horn!

"What problem?"

"The speaker of the house knows about our op in Europe. He wants me to shut it down."

"Don't worry about it. I'll take care of him."

"Make sure you do."

With a vague, "Uh huh," Forth hung up.

He looked at his secretary and said, "Now, where were we?"

CHAPTER 14

RAMSTEIN AIRFORCE BASE, GERMANY

KANE STARED hard at the man before him and tried to work out whether he was lying or not. "You're certain that the best way into the compound is by the river?"

Falk nodded and pointed at the satellite photo. "There is a place here where you should have no problems."

The assault team was gathered around looking at all the intel they had on the Latvian lab. Falk was giving them everything he knew. Axe sat in the background, a scowl on his face. Cara glanced over at him and picked up one of the photos. She walked across to him and held it out. He took it and gave her a quizzical look. "What do you want me to do with this?"

"I'm going to need a decent overwatch position, and with all of these trees, I can't seem to find one."

He grunted and said, "I'll take a look."

She smiled at him and went back to the others. When she stopped at the table, Kane said, "What was that?"

"He's working on finding me a half-decent overwatch position."

Kane nodded knowingly. "All right, we'll insert here," he stabbed the map beside the photos. "It's about two klicks out. We'll infiltrate on foot along the river until we reach the compound and cut our way in through the fence here."

"Do we know if it is electrified?" Brick asked his gaze on Falk.

"It is not."

"How many men does the place have watching over it?" Arenas asked.

"About twenty," Kane told him. "All *Jednostka Wojskowa Komandosów*. Ex-Polish Special Forces. If we go in under the cover of darkness with night vision, we should be right."

Brick pointed at a small building on its own. "What's this?"

"Power."

The ex-SEAL looked at Kane. "If we can kill, it will help."

Reaper nodded. "Fine. You do that while Carlos and I clear this building here and plant a charge in the chemical storage. We'll rendezvous at the main lab before we breach."

"Done deal."

"Once we breach the lab, we clear it and set another charge in there. Then we blow them on exfil. Cara will cover us until we're in the trees and then rendezvous with us at the fence."

Axe joined them. "Near as I can figure the best overwatch position is here."

They all looked at the position his finger indicated

and then stared at him. "That's on the other side of the river," Cara said.

"Yes, ma'am. About twelve-hundred meters. But the high ground should offer you full coverage of the target area."

"The M110A1 isn't going to cut it from that distance."

"No, ma'am. You'll need something with a bit more kick."

"If you'll allow me, ma'am, I think I might be able to find you something."

Cara looked at Kane. He nodded. "All right, get onto it."

"Hold it," Thurston said as she crossed to where they were working. "There's been a change of plan. It'll be a daytime insertion. It's all fucked up. The short version is, you'll be dropped just before dawn, and your infil will be in the lovely daylight hours."

"Damn it," Brick cursed.

Kane studied the map and pictures again. "All right, we'll insert the same way. We'll clear the first two sheds before moving on to the lab. Set charges and then exfil the same way."

Arenas shook his head. "I do not like it. With three men inside the wire, there is more chance of us getting seen. If I take up position here inside the trees, I can be an extra pair of eyes in case something happens."

"Sounds good. And if it all goes to shit, we'll have both you and Cara as overwatch."

Cara snorted. "I may as well be in the next damned country."

Axe patted her on the shoulder. "Don't worry, ma'am. I'll find you a weapon that'll put you right in the fight."

Kane said, "Now, let's talk exfil. Dropping in will be

fine. But it's been decided that we'll make for the port of Skult. We'll be picked up there by boat then brought back to Germany via sea. And before you ask about air extraction, flying a helicopter across one country and into another is not going to happen. We leave by sea."

"That's all of fifty klicks to the coast. I take it that we're not walking?" Cara asked.

"No. We'll commandeer some transport along the way."

"OK then."

"All right, everybody, check your equipment and let Cara or me know if you need anything."

———

Axe sat the suppressed sniper rifle on the table, and Cara nodded with a little more than just appreciation. "Nice. A CheyTac Intervention .408."

"Yes, ma'am. Blow a tick off a cow's ass at twenty-five hundred meters."

"Where did you steal it from?" Kane asked his friend.

Axe gave him an indignant look. "I'm hurt you would suggest such a thing."

"Where did you steal that from?" Thurston asked as she stepped in beside them.

"Now I am crushed," Axe said solemnly. "Ma'am, just because I may look the part, doesn't mean I'm such an unsavory character."

The general rolled her eyes. "That has to be the biggest load of horseshit I've heard yet."

"OK, I borrowed it from one of them air commando fellers."

"Does he know about it?"

"Yes. I told him we were headed downrange, and I had

a lovely lady who was in need of a bit more grunt than her usual M110A1. This is what he came up with. Don't get too attached to it; he wants it back."

Cara smiled. "Maybe one day. You didn't happen to get me a laser rangefinder, did you?"

"I might have got you a hand-held ballistic computer."

"OK, Axe, it's official. I'm in love with you."

A look of horror crossed his face. "Whoa, ma'am. Just slow your roll there. I'm a happily-single man."

They all chuckled. Thurston said, "Everybody get some rest. There'll be an HC-130 on the tarmac waiting for you at midnight."

"Yes, ma'am."

ABOARD THE HC-130, OVER LATVIA

Kane watched the ramp go down and waited for the light to turn green. This was the worst part. The waiting. Check that. The worst part was not knowing if your parachute would open. He shuffled forward toward the edge. Behind him came the rest of the team. He could feel his heart thudding wildly in his chest. His breathing seemed loud in the oxygen mask he wore.

They'd double-checked their equipment, and it was all good. The last pass of the satellite over the target area revealed fifteen guards. Allowing for extras, the estimation of twenty was good.

Reaper looked to his right at the loadmaster. The light beside him was still red. He held up a single finger and then crooked it. Thirty seconds.

He tugged at the straps of his parachute. All secure.

Glancing sideways at the loadmaster once again, he then counted off in his head.

The light changed to green. Kane snapped a quick salute to the loadmaster and then shuffled out into midair.

LATVIA

"Team Reaper, radio check."

"Two OK."

"Three OK."

"Five OK."

"Zero, comms check, over."

"Read you loud and clear, Reaper One," Ferrero's voice came back.

"Copy, Zero. Team Reaper, all present and correct. Moving on target, over."

"Roger, Reaper One. You're moving on target. Zero out."

The team gathered around Kane. They'd ditched their jump equipment and were now down to combat gear only. To the east, the sun was beginning to rise. It wouldn't be long until their landing area was bathed in sunlight, and Kane wanted to be far away by the time that happened.

"Brick, lead us out. The sooner we get into the trees the better. Carlos, you're rear security."

"Sí."

"All right, move out."

The river was to their left as they walked. It made a rushing sound, running over its rocky bottom. To their right was nothing but pine forest. They made good progress for the next hour before Kane called a halt. Cara came forward and knelt beside him. He said, "This is where we split off. I'll give you another hour to get in position before we infil. I'll double check before we do."

Cara nodded. "Copy."

"We'll rendezvous back here. If things go wrong and we get split up, head north toward the secondary site. Failing that, make for the coast."

"I'll see you back here."

———

CARA OVERWATCH

The river had been cold but shallow. However, the power of the rushing water had almost knocked her from her feet once. But Cara had managed to regain control and get to the far bank.

From there, the climb was relatively straight forward. Even if it was some distance away from the rest of the team. By the time she reached her hide, the sun was higher in the sky. The last part of her journey was climbing a small rock outcrop. It was flat at the top and afforded her a clear field of fire. Axe had been right.

She set up the CheyTac Intervention and lay down behind it. Cara peered through the scope and smiled. "Fantastic."

Shifting her sights downward, she searched until she found the others near the fence. Into her mic, she said, "Reaper One? Reaper Two in position, over."

"Copy, Reaper Two. How is your hide?"

"Target all clear. Axe chose well."

"Copy. Time to go to work. Reaper One, out."

———

KANE

Arenas cut through the wire just enough for them to squeeze through with their packs. They made their way through the pines until they reached the edge of the tree line. Kane said into his mic, "Reaper Two? Reaper One. How are we looking?"

"Copy, Reaper One. There are guards on the corners of buildings one and two facing the tree line. Another on the roof of building three, and I spotted a roving patrol of two on the far side of the compound."

"Copy, Reaper Two. That's going to make it difficult to get close. Wait one."

Kane looked at Arenas and Brick. "What do you guys think?"

Brick said, "With all that open area out, there it's a sure bet we'll be seen before we get to the first building."

"That was my thinking," Kane acknowledged.

"We'll have to take some of the guards out before you go in," Arenas told him. "When the patrol comes around, Cara and I can take care of them."

"All right," Kane said. Then he spoke into his mic, "Reaper Two? Reaper One. We're moving to a better position. How copy?"

"Roger, Reaper One, you're moving."

"Reaper One, out."

They circled to the left, taking their time so not to give themselves away. In the thick conifers, the dappled light filtered down, helping them stay camouflaged. Once they were in position, Kane said, "Carlos, you take building one, Brick, you're two. I'll stay as backup."

"Roger."

"Reaper Two? Reaper One. Copy?"

"Copy, Reaper One."

"I want you to hit the guy on building three on my mark. I've got Brick and Carlos down here, and they'll take the others. Once we're gone, it'll be up to you and Carlos to eliminate the roving patrol when they get around."

"Copy, Reaper One. Waiting for your mark."

"OK, you guys, tell me when you're ready."

"Three, ready."

"Five, ready."

"Two, ready."

"All right. On my mark. Three, two, one, execute."

The suppressed HK416s spat two rounds each and both guards jerked and dropped where they stood without a sound. The target on the rooftop fell a fraction behind those given the distance the bullet had to travel. All three voices came through Reaper's earpiece. "Tango down."

"OK. Good work. Brick, on me. Cara, Carlos, any problems, let me know. Don't forget the patrol."

"Copy."

Kane and Brick raised their suppressed 416s and moved forward across the open ground. They reached the first fallen man at building two and dragged him out of sight. Then they ran across to building one and did the same.

Kane and Brick halted behind the building. "Reaper Two, sitrep?"

"All clear, Reaper. It won't be long until our friends appear, but we'll take care of it."

"Copy, breaching now."

Inside were pallets stacked in rows, of formaldehyde, mercury, and ammonium chloride. All the nasty key ingredients to make ecstasy. "Bingo," Brick said in a low voice.

"Set the charges. I'll keep a lookout."

"Roger."

CARA

Cara waited patiently, scanning the compound area, looking for threats. The roving patrol was almost in position when her sweep picked up the last thing she expected to see. A young man standing outside of the lab with a cigarette jammed between his lips.

"Shit," Cara hissed in a low voice. She let the scope linger for a while as she confirmed it was who she thought. Then she pressed her talk button and said, "Reaper One? Reaper Two, copy?"

"Copy, Reaper Two."

"I just picked up our HVT, Reaper One. I say again. An HVT inside the compound."

"Confirm, Reaper Two."

"It's him, Reaper. It's Bazyli Marek."

Silence greeted her last words.

"Did you get that Reaper?"

"Copy, Reaper Two. Bazyli Marek."

RAMSTEIN AIRFORCE BASE, GERMANY

Ferrero came to his feet and signaled to Thurston. She hurried across to where he and Swift were monitoring the team's transmissions and gave him a curious look. "What is it?"

"Reaper Two has just laid eyes on Bazyli Marek."

Thurston picked up a headset and said, "Reaper Two, this is Bravo, over."

"Copy, Bravo."

"Confirm your last."

"If it isn't him, ma'am, it's his twin brother."

"Roger, Reaper Two. What's the position of the HVT?"

Cara said, "He's outside the lab, ma'am."

Thurston looked at Ferrero. "What do you think?"

"We may not get another chance."

"I agree," Thurston said with a nod. "Reaper One, copy?"

"Copy, ma'am."

"Change of mission. I want you to secure the HVT before you set the charges at the lab."

"Roger. Secure HVT then the lab. Reaper One, out."

———

CARA

Cara's voice was calm. "Three, two, one, execute."

The CheyTac Intervention slammed back against her shoulder, and the .408 round reached out the 1,238 meters to blow a fist-sized hole in the first man's head. The second man jerked as he too went down from Arenas' two well-placed shots. "Tango down."

"Reaper One, threat neutralized."

"Copy, Reaper Two. Reaper Three, copy?"

"Copy."

"I want you to join us. Once we grab the HVT, you can escort him back into the trees."

"Copy, Reaper One. Coming to you."

"Reaper Two, keep us covered."

"Roger."

KANE

"All set," Brick told Kane as he settled in beside him.

"Right. Let's go and get our man."

"Reaper Two, sitrep?"

"All clear."

The two men came out of the building and hooked right. Arenas joined them, and they all moved to the corner of the larger warehouse. Kane took a knee and surveyed the scene before him.

Marek was still outside but for how long was anyone's guess. As though on cue, he turned and walked toward the lab door.

"Reaper One, target is moving."

"I've got him, Reaper Two."

Kane turned to Arenas. "Take up position where you can cover the guard's quarters. If this goes belly up, then you can keep them pinned down and give us time."

Arenas nodded and slipped away.

Suddenly the wind picked up, making an eerie sound as it filtered through the trees. Kane said, "Are you ready, Brick?"

"I was born ready."

The two men broke cover and closed the gap to the lab door. They took up positions on either side and paused. "Try not to hit anything that might go bang," Kane said.

"That don't leave me a lot to shoot at," Brick shot back.

Reaper reached out and grasped the door handle. He

glanced at Brick who nodded. Then with a twist, the door snicked open.

Kane pushed the door, and as it swung back, he entered the building. He moved left, sweeping the room. Brick went right. The lab was full of everything required for a successful operation. From urns to pipes, and chemicals.

The first armed guard sighted by Kane was dropped with two shots. The man held an MP7 and tried to bring it up but was a week too late. Still moving, Reaper swept left and right as he went. A second guard fell from a couple of rounds from Brick's 416. Some of the workers caught sight of them and immediately fell to the hard, concrete floor.

From Brick's side, the rattle of automatic fire rang out. Silence, and then another.

"Reaper Five, sitrep."

"All good. Tango down."

"Reaper Three and Two, stand-by. You're about to get busy."

"Copy."

"Reaper One, I just spotted our HVT. Right rear corner going in behind some kind of vat."

"Copy, coming to you."

A flood of Marek's cooks flowed back past Kane as he made his way through the maze of equipment. If they didn't look to be a threat, he let them go. When he hooked up with Brick, the former SEAL said, "He's just down there. Behind that stainless-steel tub."

"Right, let's see if he's listening. Bazyli Marek! We know you're there. Come out with your hands above your head."

Nothing.

Kane raised his 416.

"What are you doing?" Brick snapped.

"Warning shot."

"Don't blow us the fuck up."

"I'll try not to."

Kane was about to squeeze the trigger when "Reaper Three engaging."

"Copy, Reaper Three," Kane acknowledged. "Brick, find a place to set your charges."

"Copy."

"Marek, last chance for you to come out. You've got two minutes, and then we blow this place sky high."

Silence.

Lifting his 416 again, Kane fired a single shot. It was enough to bring the frightened young man out from his hiding position. Bazyli had his arms raised, and he shouted, "Don't shoot!"

"Lay down on the floor," Kane barked.

The young man did as he was told, and Kane moved forward. He pulled Bazyli's hands around behind his back and used cable ties to secure them. Then he grabbed his collar and snapped, "Get the fuck up."

"You can't do this. You don't know who my father is."

Kane slapped him up the back of the head and said, "Shut up."

The team leader pushed him forward to where Brick was working. "How long?"

"One mike and we're good."

Kane pressed the transmit button on his radio. "Zero? Reaper One. Copy?"

"Copy, Reaper One."

"We have the package, Zero. We are just about to start exfil."

"Copy, Reaper One."

Brick stood up and said, "I'm done."

Kane spoke into his mic, "Reaper Two, Three, we're coming out."

Brick shoved Bazyli forward. "Move, asshole."

Once they reached the door, they could hear the rattle of gunfire a lot clearer than before. Kane opened it and peered out. He raised his 416 and let go a burst of fire at a guard who was positioned behind a crate.

"OK let's go," Kane called back over his shoulder. They slipped out the door and ran low for the first building. Once there, Kane said into the mic, "Reaper Three, disengage and fall back to me. Reaper Two, cover our exfil."

Arenas did as he was ordered, and they all regrouped behind building One. "Are you OK, Carlos?"

The Mexican nodded. "Yes. I think I accounted for two more."

"Reaper One? Reaper Two. You need to move now. Building three is regurgitating tangos."

"Copy, Reaper Two. Give us two minutes and then move to rendezvous. Carlos, lead out."

As they ran through the trees, bullets started to snap and ricochet all around them. Bark and wood splinters flew as lead gouged furrows into the pines. Cara's voice filled Kane's head, "Reaper One, you have ten tangos on your ass. Run faster."

"I've got it," Brick said and dropped back. "Let me know when you're clear."

"OK. Just keep your ass down."

The former SEAL gave him a dumb smile and slapped a fresh magazine home. "Don't leave without me."

Brick settled down behind a tree and brought his suppressed 416 up. He said into his mic, "Reaper Two, tell me a story."

"Copy, Reaper Five. How's this? Once upon a time, there were two tangos coming in on your two o'clock."

He heard the snap of the .408 round as it came in overhead. "Make that one."

"How'd you manage that?"

"I have skills, Reaper Five."

Brick smiled. He saw the second man moving through the trees and dropped him with a couple of shots to the body. "Tell me more, Reaper Two."

"Wow, this is interesting."

"What's that?"

"I have two more tangos with what looks to be an RPG, coming up on you and I have no shot."

"Copy. Where from?"

"Coming in from your eleven, Reaper Five."

Brick stared through the trees and tried to pick them up. "Reaper, you guys almost there? Things are about to heat up."

"Just about, Reaper Five."

Suddenly a rocket-propelled grenade streaked out of the forest, the telltale smoke trail indicating its path. With a loud roar, it impacted close and erupted into a ball of orange flame. Brick hugged the ground and felt the heat from it wash over him.

"Brick! Brick are you OK?" Cara's voice came over the comms.

"I'm still here, but that was close."

"Fall back before they reload."

"Copy, ma'am. Falling back."

He came to his feet and started back through the trees. An automatic rifle opened fire behind him, and he heard the rounds impact the trees. "Can you get a shot at him, ma'am?"

"Just keep your head down, Brick."

Once more Brick heard the incoming .408 round, and the rattle of the automatic fire stopped. "You won't have any more trouble with him, Reaper Five."

"Copy."

"Reaper Five? Reaper One. We're out. Fall back to the rendezvous point."

"Roger. Coming to you."

"Reaper One to all Reaper Team. Fire in the hole, I say again, fire in the hole."

Behind Brick, two large crumps could be heard followed by the accompanying fireballs which rose above the trees.

CHAPTER 15

"REAPER ONE? ZERO, OVER."

"Copy, Zero."

"Change of plans, Reaper. We've organized a chopper to come and extract the team and your package. The bad news with that is, it's twelve hours away. I'll give you some coordinates for your team to relocate to. It'll be to an LZ big enough for our purpose."

"Roger, Zero. That'll make it a nighttime op. Why the long wait?"

"General bullshit, Reaper One. The good news is that we should be able to get a satellite tasked to help out. Until then, get your team to the LZ. It'll probably take you four hours to get there. That way it's far enough out to hopefully throw off any pursuit."

"Copy, Zero. Awaiting coordinates. Reaper One, out."

"Sending now, Zero, out."

Kane gathered his team around him. "We've got air

extract coming in. The only problem is we still have to hump four hours to get to the LZ. And then we'll still have an eight-hour wait for the helo."

Brick chuckled. "Good old army."

"It is what it is. Cara, you escort our friend here and, Brick, you're on point. We'll swap around every hour."

"Where are we headed?"

"North."

———

CIA SAFEHOUSE, WARSAW, POLAND

Mark Newcomb's secure satellite phone rang and for some reason he had a feeling that it wasn't going to be a happy call. "Yeah?"

Horn's voice cut through the speaker with savage intent. "What the fuck is going on over there? I get woken up at four in the morning by Marek screaming blue fucking murder about his son."

"I'm not sure I know what you mean, sir."

"Try this on then," Horn growled. "Thurston's fucking team just blew up one of Marek's facilities in Latvia."

Newcomb glanced about the room and found Nicole. She rose from her chair when he motioned to her via hand signals that he wanted her to listen in on the call, so she worked a little magic and joined them on the line.

"And that concerns us how, sir?"

"Because they took his fucking son, that's how," Horn snarled. "Get Bull Horton and his team spun up. I want them on the ground in Latvia in three hours."

"How will we know if they're still there?" Newcomb

asked. "They could be long gone by the time Blackbird gets there."

"We're the CI fucking A, Mark. By the time the team lands we'll have a location. If they're not there, then we'll move accordingly. Now, get the team in the fucking air!"

The line went dead, and Newcomb stared across at Nicole. "Get Bull."

———

TEAM REAPER, LATVIA

They'd been on the move for two hours when the Russian built Mi-8 helicopter appeared overhead. The team went to ground in the trees and waited for it to disappear. After a couple of sweeps, it moved on to the next area. Kane called it in.

"Zero? Reaper One, over."

"Copy, Reaper One."

"Zero, it looks like Marek has air assets and they're in the air as we speak."

"What kind?"

"A Mi-8 helo."

"Copy."

"How's our back trail?"

Swift came over the net. "Reaper One? Bravo Four. The satellite picked up perhaps ten tangos about one klick back. They're keeping pace with you, not closing at all."

"What are they doing now, Bravo Four?"

"They have stopped."

"Are they shadowing us, Reaper Four?"

"That would be my guess."

Kane glanced at his team. "Slick, see if you can do a

sweep ahead of us and come up with something. I have me a feeling."

"Copy, Reaper One. Bravo Four, out."

"Is there a problem?" Cara asked.

"Yes, we're being herded like cattle. I've a feeling that we're about to run into something ahead of us."

"Any idea what?"

"Not a damned clue."

Kane got the team moving through the trees again. Arenas was on point, and they'd covered half a klick when Swift came over the comms. "Reaper One? Bravo Four, copy?"

"Copy, Bravo Four."

"OK, so your friends are moving again, and I've done a sweep ahead of you, and it looks clear. However, I did some sniffing around to try and find out what our friends at the CIA are up to. They flew a new team in after you took out the other one. This one is a little different. It's Bull Horton's Blackbird Team."

"Copy that. Do you happen to know where they are?"

"They took off from Warsaw-Modlin Airport around two and a half hours ago."

"No prizes for guessing where they're headed."

"That's what we figured."

"What time frame are we looking at?"

"They should be on the ground in around thirty minutes."

"Copy. Get Zero for me, Reaper One, out."

"Roger. Out."

Kane said to his team, "You guys get all that?"

They nodded. Cara asked, "Who's Bull Horton."

Brick said, "He heads up a Delta team that the CIA use all the time. They're damned good at what they do, so I've heard."

"They're more than good," Kane said. "In the world of SPECOPS, they're considered the best."

"You meet him, Reaper?" Brick asked.

"Yeah, few years back."

Before they could talk anymore, the comms came to life. "Reaper One? Zero, over."

"Copy, Zero. The team and I are going to take a little detour. We'll head east a couple of klicks and lay up until we think it's all clear. That way we can make the rendezvous with the helo when required."

"Roger that, Reaper One. The word from Bravo is do not engage unless you have to. Over."

"Good copy, Zero. Reaper One, out."

The team gathered around Kane, and they looked over the map. He touched an area and said, "Looks like there's some high ground here and trees to go with it. We'll lay up there until it's time to head out to the LZ. Hopefully, Horton and his team will slide right by. Any questions?"

They all shook their heads.

"I have one?" Bazyli said.

Kane looked at him and said, "Shut the fuck up."

———

RAMSTEIN AIRFORCE BASE, GERMANY

Back in Ramstein, Axe paced back and forth around the hangar as he waited for reports to come in. He'd been on edge when they hit the compound, and that had eased some since they'd extracted afterward. However, the intel that Bull Horton and Blackbird were inbound set him on edge once more.

"Where are they now?" he asked Swift for the

hundredth time.

The computer tech pointed at the screen and said, "Right there. They've moved a hundred meters further on from their last position. Take a load off and relax, man. You're starting to freak me out."

Axe walked away from Swift and heard him say, "Here we go."

The ex-recon marine turned and hurried back. "Here we go, what?"

"Reaper One? Bravo Four, over."

"Copy, Bravo Four."

"You've just had a helicopter touch down about two klicks to your northeast."

"Copy, Bravo Four. Keep me informed."

Axe watched on the screen as figures were disgorged from the helicopter. Marvelous things satellites. He counted twelve men, no doubt wearing full tactical gear. They took all of thirty seconds to disembark, and then the helo lifted off again.

"Axe, you got a minute?" Thurston called out from across the hangar.

He walked over to her and said, "Yes, ma'am?"

"Can you and Traynor take Falk back to the lockup? I dismissed his guard a while back because he was cooperating with us and he wasn't a threat."

Axe looked over at the manufacturer. He was sitting patiently at the interrogation table.

"Yes, ma'am."

"Thank you."

He walked over to the table and said, "Time to go home."

The man nodded and stood up. Traynor came over to join them. "We all good to go?"

"Sure are."

They began to escort him to toward the door when it opened, and four armed men in BDUs entered. "Who are you guys?" Traynor asked them.

"We're here to escort the prisoner back," a tall man said.

Axe shrugged. "That's where we were going."

Two of them unslung their MP7s. "We'll take him."

"Sure. Here you go."

The four men took possession of Falk and started toward the door. Axe said to Traynor, "You ever know MPs to carry MP7s before?"

Traynor looked at him. "Shit, Axe, I don't know."

"Let me tell you this," he said. "They don't."

He brought up his M17 and said in a loud voice, "Hey, you fucked up."

The leader turned around and saw the gun. "What the hell, man?"

"MPs don't carry MP7s."

Sudden realization registered on the man's face and he tried to bring his gun into play. The M17 crashed, and the intruder was flung back. Axe shifted his aim and put two into the next man in the line.

Taken by surprise, Traynor was a little slower than Axe. By the time the third man took a bullet in his chest from the former DEA agent, his MP7 was almost level. An involuntary jerk of the trigger finger sprayed bullets throughout the hangar, sending those within ducking for cover.

Axe accounted for the last shooter. Two shots. One to the chest and the other to the throat. The man dropped to the concrete floor and bled out.

"You clear?" Axe snapped to Traynor.

"Yes. Clear."

"Check them. I'll take a look outside. Falk, are you OK?"

Falk was huddled on the floor in the position he'd taken when the first shots were fired. "I'm OK," came his muffled reply.

While Axe went outside, Traynor checked the fallen shooters. All were beyond help, but he kicked their weapons away anyway. Force of habit and good practice.

"What the hell just happened here?" Thurston asked, her voice elevated. Behind her came Ferrero.

"These guys came here for a reason, but we don't know why," Traynor explained. "But they sure as shit are not MPs."

He went on and explained what happened and how Axe picked up that they were imposters.

"Christ!" Thurston cursed. "Whoever did this has got some fucking balls. Slick? Where are you?"

"Here, ma'am," came the reply and the tech hurried over.

"Get some pictures of these bastards and find out who they are," the general snarled.

"Yes, ma'am. But that might be a bit hard."

She glared at him. "Say that again."

"That burst of fire that ripped through the hangar, ma'am. A couple of rounds smashed into our station. We've got no electronics at this point in time."

"Fuck!" she hissed.

"It gets worse, ma'am. We've got no communications with Kane and his team. For the time being, they're on their own."

Thurston stared at Ferrero. "Luis, get this cleaned up. I'll be back as soon as I can get us some equipment."

BLACKBIRD TEAM, LATVIA

The sound of the helicopter disappeared into the distance, the whop-whop-whop of its rotor lost to the valley. Bull Horton pressed the transmit button on his comms. "Blackbird on Station. Comms check, over."

"Copy, Blackbird. Read you loud and clear. Your target is approximately two klicks southwest of your position."

"Copy, Blackbird Base. Moving to target."

Horton turned to his number two and said, "Set your course to the southwest. You're on point. Two klicks."

The man nodded and disappeared into the trees.

Horton turned and looked at his team. They were good, professional. He'd been in many hot zones with all of them. This was just another day.

"Blackbird Team, move out."

———

TEAM REAPER, LATVIA

"Zero? Reaper One, how copy?"

Static.

"Zero? Reaper One, how copy?"

More static.

"Nothing?" asked Cara.

Kane shook his head. He'd been trying for the past hour to get an update on Horton's Blackbird Team, but Ramstein had remained eerily silent.

"I don't like it," he said to Cara. "They've been quiet too long."

"The question is, why?"

Kane nodded. They'd arrived at their lay up about ten

minutes beforehand. He'd posted Carlos as rear guard and sent Brick to have a look around. He hated being blind, but it wouldn't be the first time. He said, "Make sure our friend is secure."

"Roger that."

Brick returned a couple of minutes later, roughly an hour before the sun would be gone. He slipped through the trees and was suddenly there.

"What did you find?" Kane asked.

"There's a small house and barn about a klick to our north. It's surrounded by open ground. The barn looks solid enough, so does the house for that matter."

"Did you see anyone there?"

"No. The place looks deserted."

Kane thought for a moment and then said into his mic, "Cara, on me. Reaper Three, fall back."

A few moments later they were gathered around him in the stand of trees they'd taken refuge in. He said, "Brick found a deserted farm or some such about a klick to our north. It has a good field of fire around it, so we're going to fall back there. I still can't raise Ramstein so we're flying blind and, in these trees, we can't see what's coming. At least we'll be able to see them coming across open fields. Plus, with a bit of luck, it'll be dark by then anyway. Any questions?"

Cara said, "What's our field of fire?"

Brick said, "Three hundred meters in all directions."

"Then why can't we redirect our extract to there?"

Kane nodded. It made sense. "If we get our comms back with Bravo, I'll suggest it. All right, Brick. Lead us out."

When the team reached the edge of the tree line, they paused, and Kane glanced at Cara. "Scope."

She raised the .408 and swept the target before them.

First the house and then the barn. Neither showed signs of life. "I can't see anything, Reaper."

"OK. Set up here for the moment with Brick. Carlos and I will go on in and have a look."

The two of them moved forward out of the dense trees and into the lush field. The grass showed no sign of recent grazing for it was almost up to their knees. Their approach was smooth and deliberate, sweeping left and right, looking for any indication of trouble.

Once Kane and Arenas reached the main building, they split up. While the Mexican went around to the front, the Team Reaper commander tried the back door. It swung open, and Kane let the 416 hang from its shoulder strap, and he took out his M17, raised it, and stepped inside.

It smelled musty, unused. There was also the smell of mice and possibly something dead. Searching rooms as he went, Kane met up with Arenas in the living room. "No one has been here for a long time, *amigo*," Arenas said.

"It would seem that way. Plenty of furniture. Seems like whoever was here just walked out."

The Mexican nodded at the floor near the fire. "They forgot something when they did."

Kane looked at the foul looking mat and saw the source of the room's odor. A dead cat or it had once been a cat, but time had taken its toll on the animal's corpse.

"I guess that's the dead smell," he pointed out. "Let's check the barn."

Suddenly Kane's comms crackled to life. "Reaper One? Zero. How copy?"

"Loud and clear, Zero. What happened? We're blind as a bat out here."

"We had issues, Reaper. Still do. We have our comms back up, but we've no eye in the sky. All we know is that

Horton's Blackbird Team was headed in your direction before we lost the feed. *Not* towards your old location but an intercept course. At the moment, I can't help you with any more."

"Copy, Zero. I do have a request. Can you reroute the helo to these coordinates? It's an abandoned farm with good LZs all around."

"Wait one, Reaper," Ferrero said, and the comms went quiet.

Kane and Arenas moved out of the house and walked over to the barn. Inside smelled of stale straw, old animal crap, and dust. The best part about it was the loft where Cara could set up a sniper nest.

"Reaper One? Bravo, over."

"I'm here, ma'am."

"Zero tells me you're requesting alternate extract. Is that right?"

"Roger, Bravo. Can you do it?"

"Affirmative, Reaper, I'll set it up. Bravo, out."

Kane walked out of the barn and looked toward the tree line. "Reaper Two? Reaper One. Come on in."

CHAPTER 16

WHEN DARK DESCENDED over the Latvian landscape, the team broke out their NVGs, but Kane made sure that all laser sights were switched off on the 416s. Cara was up in the loft doing regular sweeps at both ends of the barn with her night-vision scope. So far there was nothing to report which made Kane happy. He looked at the illuminated face of his watch. Two hours until the helo arrived.

Kane sat with his back against a square post. Across from him, he could make out the shadowy form of Bazyli. "Why did you do it?" Kane asked him.

"Do what?"

"Put the tab in the drink that killed the girl?"

"I don't know what you mean."

"Fuck off, Bazyli, you were caught on camera."

He hesitated. "I didn't know it would kill her. She was pretty; I thought it might loosen her up a little."

"You mean you were using it to try and get into her

pants," Kane stated bluntly. "Drug them and get them as high as a kite so they can't say no? Is that it?"

"No."

"Bullshit."

"Is this why you come all this way from America? To get me?"

Kane chuckled. "It's not all about you, you prick. We came for one of our friends and decided to pay your old man's factory a visit. Put a dent in his operations. You were just a bonus."

"How did you know it was there?"

Kane ignored the question. "I have a friend in Ramstein who's just waiting to meet you. Somehow, I think you'll be lucky to get out of there alive. The girl you killed was his sister."

"I did not mean for her to die," Bazyli snapped.

"Too fucking bad. You'll go back to the States, and you'll be tried for murder. Maybe even get your own little cocktail straight into your arm."

Marek remained silent.

Kane's comms crackled to life in his ear. "Reaper One? Bravo Four, copy?"

"Good copy, Bravo Four."

"Reaper, I've got visual back up, and it's telling me you have some friends about to knock on your door from the south and the north. Two groups."

Kane came to his feet. "Give me numbers, Bravo Four."

"Approximately ten to the south and a further twelve tangos to the north," Swift informed him. "The ones to the north will no doubt be Bull Horton's team."

"Can you confirm that the helo is still an hour out?"

"Affirmative."

"Roger. Keep me up to date. Reaper One out."

Kane walked to the north end of the barn. He cracked one of the sliding wood doors and stared out into the darkness, illuminated a pale green by his NVGs. "Cara, you got anything?"

"Not yet, Reaper."

"They're out there somewhere."

Kane traversed the barn to the other end where Arenas and Brick were stationed. "You guys got anything?"

"Not yet," Arenas told him.

"Keep an eye out; they're coming in. But don't fire until I give the all clear. And no lasers until then either. They'll have night-vision."

"Reaper?" Cara's voice wasn't much more than a whisper over the comms. "I've got movement to the north."

"Copy. On my way."

Kane moved swiftly across the barn to the doors. He looked through the gap and said, "Whereabouts, Cara?"

"There's two of them coming forward from the tree line. About twenty meters apart."

"OK. I've got them."

They were coming in low and slow. Being cautious. Kane figured there would be a team sniper back in the trees somewhere out of sight. He pressed the transmit button on his comms. "Reaper Two, watch for a sniper back there in the trees."

"Copy."

"Let them come in. If they get too close, I'll take them. Don't expose yourself yet until we know if there's a long-range shooter out there."

"Roger that."

Kane kept low and watched through a crack in the door. The two shooters kept on coming. Using the darkness to their advantage. They were dressed in black and moved like silent wraiths floating over the ground. When they were still a hundred meters out, two more appeared.

Kane's comms crackled to life. "Reaper, we have two more coming in."

"Copy, Reaper Two," he acknowledged. Then, "Bravo Four? Reaper One, sitrep, over."

"Reaper One, you have four closing from the north..."

"I've got them, Bravo Four."

"And there are two more teams of two circling to the left and right. I guess they're trying to box you in."

"Which would mean they know we're here," Kane proposed.

"Roger that."

"Back in those trees. Is there sign of a shooter who hasn't moved in a long while?"

"Wait one."

"Team, keep an eye out to the east and west, we've got flankers."

"Copy."

"Reaper One, copy?"

"Go ahead, Bravo Four."

"I found a shooter at your one o'clock who has remained on station since they arrived. If I had to bet, he's the guy you're looking for."

"Copy. Reaper One out. Cara, you get that?"

"Looking for him now."

Kane focused his attention back out through the crack in the door. The dark figures floating in the sea of green were closer again. He brought up his 416 and waited for a little more time. The shooters were within fifty meters now and still coming toward them. Kane pressed the talk button on his comms. "Reaper Two, have you found that sniper yet?"

"I think so."

Fuck. "You think so?"

"Yes."

"On my mark I want you to take a shot at him. I'd prefer you to hit him but just getting it close will do."

"Copy, Reaper One. On your mark."

Kane reached down and switched on his laser sights, making sure to keep it hidden behind the door. Then he placed himself in position and opened the doors of the barn wide enough for him to fire through.

"Three, two, one, execute."

He heard the slap of the CheyTac as he dropped the laser sight on the first of the two shooters. He fired twice, shifted aim, and fired twice more. Then he dropped to the floor of the barn just as a round from the sniper in the trees came in and blew a board off the barn door not far from where he'd fired from.

"I don't think you got him, Reaper Two."

The CheyTac fired again, and Cara said, "I did that time."

The death of the three shooters seemed to rip a hole in the night from which was released a hailstorm of lead. The exterior of the barn was peppered by relentless gunfire which made it sound like a thousand hammers being pounded on the wall boards.

Out there somewhere one of Horton's men had an M249 Light Machinegun that slammed round after round through the thin skin of the barn. Kane crawled to the doors and started to lay down his own fire.

The two of Horton's men who were coming in behind the first pair had gone to ground and from their prone position were sending deliberate fire into the team's sanctuary.

Kane fired a couple of outward rounds and then

pressed the button on his comms. "Brick, Carlos, watch the flanks. They'll try to keep us pinned down, and then they'll hit us."

"Copy, Reaper."

To his front, Kane saw one of the shooters start to move to his left. He put a couple of 5.56 rounds in his direction and saw him go to ground. Up above, he heard the CheyTac fire again and then the firing seemed to get heavier.

"Fuck it," Kane hissed as a slug blew splinters into his face. The sting told him that he'd been cut at least once from a razor-sharp sliver. He flicked the selector switch to auto and blew off the remainder of the magazine at the still prone figures.

Drawing back from the doorway, he took another magazine from his webbing and slapped it home. He then paused to say into his mic, "Bravo Four, sitrep on the second team of shooters, over?"

"Copy, Reaper One. They look like they're about to engage from the south."

"How far out is the helo?"

"Still at least twenty mikes."

"Shit."

"Say again, Reaper One."

"Copy, Bravo Four. Out."

Keeping low because of the bullets still punching through the wall boards, Kane hurried across to the eastern side of the barn and looked out the window. Below it, he tested the boards and found a couple of loose ones. Then with a powerful kick, they came away, and he'd made a hole big enough for a person to fit through.

From outside, Kane heard the loud crump of an explosion, the concussive blast rattling the entire structure. His head twisted on his shoulders and he could see the orange ball of fire through the cracks.

Cara's voice crackled over his comms, the urgency in it evident. "Reaper, they've got a 203 out there somewhere."

The M203 was a single-shot 40mm grenade launcher that was slung under an assault weapon. It had a range of four-hundred meters, and in the right hands, it was deadly.

"Reaper One to Reaper Team. Fall back on me. I say again, fall back on me, we're getting out of here."

Another explosion blew the double-doors wide open, and the fireball ignited the straw on the floor near them. Kane rushed across to where Bazyli was tied. "Come on, asshole, get up."

There was no response, so Kane looked closer and found him to be dead. "Fuck it."

Arenas and Brick were the first to join him. He pointed at the hole in the wall and shouted, "Out that way. We're leaving."

Just as they were disappearing, Cara arrived. "Follow Brick and Carlos. We're getting out."

"What about the package?"

"He's dead. Now move."

They pushed out through the hole and saw Arenas and Brick moving toward the tree line. Kane said, "This is going to be the longest fucking three hundred meters ever."

They'd gone no further than fifty of those when the barn blew up from a grenade round. Boards blew outwards, and the roof collapsed. The surrounding area lit up from the explosion, and the four escapees dove into the grass. When the illumination subsided, the team was back up and running once more.

Their withdrawal had not gone unnoticed, and the air

was soon filled with the buzz of a swarm of angry lead hornets as the shooters shifted fire. Kane paused his rapid retreat briefly to exchange fire, burning through half a magazine before continuing.

Ahead of him, he heard a shout. Christ! They'd run straight for the shooters sent to flank them. Arenas and Brick stopped and unleashed on the tree line. Steadily they began walking forward, issuing small bursts of suppressing fire as they went. One of the hidden shooters cried out after a lucky round punched through his leg.

"Loading!" The shout came from Brick as he ejected an empty magazine and then slapped another home. Kane and Cara pushed forward to lend fire support. Cara was using her M17, the CheyTac now hanging from a strap over her shoulder.

Bullets whipped around them, emanating from every direction, burning holes in the nighttime air. How they'd evaded death so far was anyone's guess. But lady luck held firm, and they were soon amongst the relative safety of the trees.

"Keep moving," Kane snapped.

Ahead of him, he saw Brick put down the second of the two shooters with a shot to the head. The wounded one, though down, was not out and still posed a threat, so he met the same fate as his fellow operator. As difficult as it was, the notion that they were here to kill them was a reminder that it was their only option.

"Reaper Team, check-in," Kane said into his mic.

"Two OK."

"Four OK."

"Five OK."

"Keep moving to your twelve o'clock," Kane said. "Stop for nothing."

"Roger, I have point," Arenas told him.

"Zero? Reaper One, copy?"

"Copy, Reaper One."

"I need a new LZ."

"Copy. How's the package?"

"He's dead."

"Roger. Wait one, we'll get back to you."

"Copy, out."

BLACKBIRD, LATVIA

Bull Horton was one pissed commander. The assault had cost him six men. Half his fucking force. Christ! All for nothing. The team he'd been tasked to terminate had gotten away without so much as a scratch, and now they'd disappeared into the darkness. And what had happened to the other force? The ex-*Jednostka Wojskowa Komandosów* that were meant to push in from the south and give them a hand.

"I found him for you, Bull," the black-clad man said as he came from the dark.

Horton turned to face the man and said in an angry voice, "What the fuck happened to you and your men?"

"You attacked before we were ready," the man said in broken English.

"You should have been in fucking position, you useless clod. You cost me six good men."

"It was not my fault. If you waited, then it would be different."

"Well, fuck you too," Horton snarled. "They got away to the east. Get your men out there and start tracking them. My team will bring up the rear. I'll not waste more of their lives because you're fucking incompetent."

The man mumbled something in his own language and disappeared back into the darkness.

"Blackbird Base to Blackbird One, over."

"Copy, Blackbird Base."

"What's going on, Bull?" Newcomb asked. "You've been sitting there for at least twenty minutes while Kane and his team gets away."

"I lost six fucking men in that shitstorm, Newcomb. I'm not about to risk the rest of my team by chasing them around in the dark."

"We still have eyes on them, Bull."

"Good. Guide the Poles into position. Use them as cannon fodder. Blackbird out."

"What do you want us to do, Bull?" asked a man who'd brought the Pole in.

"Have everyone remain at least a hundred meters behind the last man in the Polish line. No closer than that."

"Roger."

———

TEAM REAPER, LATVIA

"Reaper One? Zero. Copy?"

"Copy, Zero."

"Reaper, about one klick to the north of your current position is a clearing big enough to put a Black Hawk down. You'll need to hustle because you have tangos closing on your six."

"Roger, Zero. Reaper One, out," Kane acknowledged and then said, "Step it up, Brick. We've got tangos on our ass."

"Copy."

For the next twenty minutes, traversing the terrain at as quick a clip as it allowed, they reached the clearing, and Kane had them form a defensive line to repel of advance of their pursuers.

Then they waited.

Five minutes later the steady throb of rotor blades started to build from the west. A voice crackled through Kane's comms. "Reaper One, this is Cherokee One-One, copy? Over."

"Cherokee One-One? Reaper One. Hear you loud and clear, over."

"Roger, Reaper One, we're about two mikes out from the new LZ. How's it looking?"

"All quiet at the moment, Cherokee One-One. I wouldn't take too long though. We have tangos closing on our position."

"Copy."

The sound of the Black Hawk grew louder, and soon it flared overhead and began its descent toward them. Suddenly the night erupted with gunfire and bullets started to hammer at the helo.

"Damn it," Kane heard the pilot say over his comms. "Cherokee One-One coming out. It's too hot. Will do a sweep before we come back in."

"Get some fire into those trees," Reaper snapped, and soon his team was laying down a carpet of gunfire trying to suppress the incoming rounds.

Overhead the Black Hawk pivoted on an invisible point, and the minigun in the doorway came ripping into life. Tracers lit up the night and disappeared into the forest. The audible sound of 7.62 caliber bullets slapping into the trees could be heard over the noise of the rotor blades.

The helicopter banked away and did a sweep over the

area, its guns not letting up. Once the run was complete, the pilot's voice came back over the comms. "Have your people ready, Reaper One, this will be a hot extract."

"Roger, Cherokee One-One."

The Black Hawk roared back in over the LZ and dropped heavily to the ground. No sooner had its wheels touched down when Team Reaper broke cover and ran toward it.

Clambering aboard, Reaper shouted, "Last man!" and the Black Hawk powered into the sky.

"Welcome aboard, Reaper One. We'll have you home in no time."

"Thanks for the ride, Cherokee, you couldn't have arrived at a better time."

"Check that," the co-pilot's voice came over the radio. "Looks like we've got a bogey inbound from the south."

Up front, the pilot said, "Confirm."

The co-pilot came back over the comms and said, "Confirm tango. It's a Hind-D incoming. Shall we engage?"

"Let's figure out his intentions first."

The Hind came swooping in for a pass to the rear of the Black Hawk. As it did its minigun opened fire.

"OK, his intentions are clear," the Black Hawk's pilot snapped, putting the helicopter into a steep bank. "Hang on back there, Reaper One. It's time to have some fun with this clown. Door gunners, weapons free."

As the helicopter banked steeply, the passengers grabbed hold of anything they could find. The gunners, however, kept hold of their weapons, their night vision searching the stygian darkness of the sky for their target.

The pilot's voice came back over the net and Kane heard him say, "Tango coming back in on port side. Get ready, Pinky."

"Copy, skipper, let me at him."

The minigun opened fire and Kane could see the illuminated fingers of the tracer rounds reaching out across
the sky through the open doorway. Then he saw the
Hind's own tracers light up and lance toward them.

The Black Hawk shuddered under the bullet strikes,
and there was a shout as the gunner named Pinky was hit.
He lurched away from his weapon and fell onto his back.
The door gunner opposite immediately cried out over the
comms. "Pinky's hit! Pinky's hit!"

"How bad?" asked the pilot in a calm voice.

"I'm not sure."

Brick lurched forward from his seated position and
started to work on the fallen crew member. Kane said into
his comms, "We've got this Cherokee. One of my men is a
medic. You just keep flying."

"Copy, Reaper. You don't have a door gunner with
you at all?"

"I'll see what I can find."

He glanced at Cara and pointed to the minigun. She
nodded and scrambled around Brick and the wounded
Pinky to take up position.

"Door gunner up," she said over the comms.

"Roger that," the pilot said. "The Hind is coming
back around on the port side. He's all yours."

The tracer from the attacking helicopter lit up the sky
once more, and the pilot jinked the Black Hawk away
from the incoming rounds. Cara let loose with the
minigun and her own tracers sprayed outward.

"Fuck!" Kane heard her hiss through her comms.

A voice came over the net. Kane assumed it was the
co-pilot. "Use the tracers to guide you onto the target
ma'am. Remember you have to lead him. It's a little
different from shooting at people."

The Hind swooped in behind the Black Hawk, and the sound of bullets on the fuselage made Kane think of a hail storm. Some of them punched through the skin of the helicopter, and he was sure he felt the passing of one round close to his face.

The door gunner on the starboard side opened up with his minigun, and a long brrrrrp sounded like thick fabric being ripped apart.

More bullets streaked out of the night, this time they missed. The pilot's voice filled Cara's head when he said, "Coming around to the port side. Get ready."

The Hind started to slide past the Black Hawk, and as it did, Cherokee seemed to edge his helicopter closer. The minigun's barrels began to rotate, and fire erupted from each muzzle as it came around. Cara saw the deadly fingers of light reach out and strike the Hind a savage blow. It seemed to stagger in the air and then slowly drop away beneath them.

"Good shooting," the pilot said over the radio. "He's going down."

An orange glow flared in the darkness behind them, illuminating the tall trees where the bird had crashed. Cara turned and stared at Kane through her NVGs. He nodded at her and pressed his transmit button. "Are you OK?"

She nodded and looked to where Brick was working on the downed door gunner. "Better than him."

CHAPTER 17

LANGLEY, VIRGINIA

"YOU ARE FUCKING KIDDING ME," Horn hissed into the handset. "Are you people totally incompetent?"

On the other end of the call, Newcomb was silent. "You lose half of the best black ops team the CIA have, your target gets away, and to top it off, Marek's son is killed. Did I miss anything the fuck out?"

"You forgot the part about the helicopter getting shot down," Newcomb said.

"Fuck you, Mark."

"Yes, sir."

"What now, Mark? Do I send you half the National Guard to see if you can get them killed too?"

"We'll take care of it, sir."

"Make sure you damned well do," Horn snarled and slammed the phone down.

———

CIA SAFEHOUSE, WARSAW, POLAND

Newcomb stared at the satellite phone for a long time before he put it down. Nicole watched him for a moment before saying, "Didn't take it well, I gather?"

"Bad news is seldom received well."

A computer tech approached Newcomb, holding a piece of paper. "Something you need to see, sir. I think it may be something we can use."

Newcomb took it and read through the sheet slowly. Then he passed it across to Nicole. After she'd finished with it, she looked at her boss and asked, "What do you think?"

"I think we need to redeploy our team."

———

RAMSTEIN AIRFORCE BASE, GERMANY—THAT SAME TIME

Mary Thurston took a pull from her beer bottle and sat it back on the table she was using as her desk. Sitting across from her was Ferrero, a frosty beer in his hands. Thurston fingered her bottle and said, "Just what I need to be doing. Drinking beer in the early hours of the morning after an op goes sideways."

"It wasn't a total waste," Ferrero pointed out. "We still did what we aimed to do. I'm sure Axe won't be disappointed that the person responsible for his sister's death is dead."

Thurston nodded. "What do you think we should do next?"

"You're asking me?"

"I am."

"We've come this far. How about we go after the head of the snake?"

The general studied him. "I'd like to, but I might have to run it past Hank first."

"OK. While Slick has had some downtime, I've had him digging around into the affairs of Marek."

"Has he found anything useful that might be used to our advantage?"

"Not that I'm aware of. But if there is, he'll find it."

And find it he did.

Thurston looked up to see Swift approaching them from across the hangar. She nodded in his direction. "Shouldn't he be racked out?"

Ferrero swiveled his head and saw Swift. "He should be."

When he reached them, Thurston growled, "Why aren't you getting some sleep? The team won't be back before dawn."

Swift shrugged. "I was too switched on, ma'am. So, I thought I'd put my awake hours to some good use."

Thurston noticed the sheets of paper he held in his hand. "What's that?"

"I was trying to work out a way we could hit Marek where it really hurts. So, I did a little digging into his finances. Apparently, he has an account in a Swiss bank. He visits Geneva once a month with another man. The number belongs to a safety deposit box. The other man goes there at least once a week for the same amount of time."

"What do they do with a safety deposit box for an hour?" Thurston asked.

"I'm not sure, yet."

Ferrero looked at Swift thoughtfully. "Do you have a picture of the other man?"

The computer tech smiled. He handed them a sheet of paper containing a picture. They studied the image, glancing at each other before looking at the big shit-eating grin on Swift's face. Thurston said, "I want that prick in here first thing. He's got some fucking explaining to do."

RAMSTEIN AIRFORCE BASE, GERMANY

Team Reaper got off the Black Hawk soon after dawn, walked into the hangar, dumped their gear, and lay down on the hard floor beside it, spent.

Kane breathed deeply as he tried to relax, come down. Beside him, Cara said, "Remind me not to carry a cannon on the next mission."

"Too much gun for you?"

They both opened their eyes to see the big ex-recon marine staring down at them. Cara shook her head. "Nice gun, just weighs a ton when you're humping it downrange."

"I heard you had some fun while we were out," Kane said.

"Nothing I couldn't handle. The boss wants you to get cleaned up and sleep for a while. She's got something else in the wind. I don't know what it is, but she seemed mighty excited about it."

Arenas joined the conversation. "Axe, fuck off. I'm staying right here."

Kane gave a wry smile. "What he said."

Axe shrugged. "I try to be nice, and this is what I get."

"Axe," Cara joined in. "I still love you, but..."

He nodded. "Yes, ma'am."

Kane dragged himself into a vertical position, then

helped the others. He said, "Get your gear sorted and then shower. After that, sleep. All in that order."

Axe said, "Leave your weapons, I'll clean them for you."

Kane slapped him on the back. "Thanks, buddy."

———

While the team rested, Pete Traynor and Mary Thurston waited for their prisoner to return. A little after eight, he was escorted into the hangar by Ferrero and Reynolds who'd driven over to the Ramstein lockup and retrieved him.

Falk assumed his usual position at the interrogation table. Thurston said to Ferrero, "Did you tell him anything?"

"No."

"Fine," she turned to Traynor. "You ready?"

"Oh, yeah."

Crossing to the table, they stood behind the two chairs, staring at Falk. After a minute, he was starting to become uncomfortable at the scrutiny and squirmed in his seat. Ten seconds later Thurston said, "You tried to fuck us. Personally, I don't mind the odd bit of horizontal calisthenics. I'm sure Pete here doesn't either. But when you try to stick that pencil dick of yours in our asses, we've got a fucking problem."

"What?"

Thurston dropped the photo of Falk and Marek onto the table. Glancing at it briefly, he was unable to hide the flicker of recognition in his eyes. Traynor growled, "You forgot to tell us about that, Falk. That maybe it slipped your mind, is what I thought at first. But then I got to thinking, how could you forget it? You know what I came up with? You are fucked. Not just you, but your family too. You tried to screw us, well, you truly screwed them."

"No, wait."

"Talk, asshole," Traynor growled. "What goes on there?"

"Bookkeeping."

Thurston and Traynor glanced at each other. The latter said, "What do you mean?"

Falk hesitated. "The agreement?"

"That's up to you," Thurston said. "At the moment I'm tempted to rip it up."

"No, don't."

"Well, you'd better make this good."

"Before I manufactured drugs, I was also an accountant," Falk explained.

The questioning looks on his interrogator's faces caused him to add, "Drugs pay better."

They nodded, and he continued. "Every week I go to Switzerland and fill out the *grootboek*. Ledger."

"What kind of ledger?" Thurston asked.

"Money, business, accounts, things like that."

"Banking details?" Traynor asked.

"Yes."

The former DEA agent turned to his commander. "We could use this, ma'am."

Thurston nodded. She said, "The question is, how do we get it?"

Traynor shrugged, "We could always rob a bank."

––––––––

"The hell you say," Kane said in wonderment. "Sorry, ma'am, but yeah. That's downright crazy."

He glanced at Cara who nodded. "I agree. We slip into a neutral country and rob one of their banks."

"We're not robbing, robbing it. We're using Falk to get in there and open the box."

Kane glanced around the others who stood at the table. Falk remained silent, as did Traynor. After all, it was his idea. He said to his team, "What do you think?"

Cara said, "How about we hear the rest of the plan first."

Kane stared at Traynor. "It's your idea."

"It's as simple as walking in the front door and accessing the box. Falk should have no problem there."

The Team Reaper commander looked at the silent man. "Is it that simple?"

He nodded. "In theory. I do it all the time."

Kane nodded. "What about backup?"

Thurston said, "I'm shifting the whole team in-country. You and Brick will accompany Falk into the bank while Cara, Carlos, and Axe will be outside in a second vehicle. Remember that there will be a lot of civilian traffic inside. If something happens, you can't do anything until it moves outside."

Shifting his gaze to Swift, Kane asked his next question. "Are you able to work your magic for us?"

The tech nodded. "I can get eyes inside, monitor police traffic, and anything else we might need eyes on."

"Reaper," Ferrero said. "I don't like it either, and I'm not going to order you to do it. It's up to you and your team."

Kane said, "Show of hands."

Each team member raised their hand.

"OK, then. It looks like we're a go."

———

GENEVA, SWITZERLAND

It took twenty-four hours for the team to get packed up and flown covertly into Switzerland. Thurston and Ferrero found an abandoned warehouse with the power still switched on, that suited their needs. The equipment transferred from Ramstein was minimal. It had to be because there was no way they could land a C-17 at the airport. Thurston's contacts were able to provide three black Range Rovers for them to use, two of which were situated outside the bank where Marek kept his ledger.

It was now almost two in the afternoon and Cara, Axe, and Arenas were sitting across the busy street from the big, five-floor structure with large windows delineating each level. They watched Falk walking toward the large double-glazed doors of the main entrance, flanked by Kane and Brick. A big sign above the doors read, **Deutsche Bank der Schweiz**.

They had almost reached them when Arenas snapped into his comms, "Abort! Abort!"

Immediately they saw Kane and the others walk to their right, away from the bank's entry.

"What is it?" Cara asked urgently.

Arenas pointed to a white Mercedes SUV on the opposite side of the road, maybe fifty meters distant. "There. I can make out at least two people in it. They haven't moved. If you look three cars back, you'll see another."

"Got them," Cara snapped.

"Talk to me, Reaper Two," Kane's voice came over the comms.

"Wait one, Reaper," she said, then, "Bravo, we may have a problem."

"Copy, Reaper Two," Ferrero said calmly. "What is it?"

"I have two white Mercedes SUVs on the street. Possibly not friendly."

"Copy, Reaper Two. Wait one."

"Talk to me, Cara," Reaper said.

"Looks like we could have friends, Reaper. You need to keep an eye out for others."

"Copy."

About a minute later Swift came over the comms. "Reaper Two, copy?"

"Copy, Bravo Four."

"I found your two vehicles plus another two for a total of four."

"Color on the other two?" Cara asked.

"Black. One is three cars back behind your position, and the other is across the street almost where Reaper is."

"Shit," Cara hissed under her breath. "Reaper did you get that?"

"Copy."

"What do you want to do?"

"I'm thinking that the safest place is in that damned bank."

Although he couldn't see, Cara nodded and looked at Axe and Arenas. Both agreed. Ferrero said, "Are you sure about that, Reaper?"

"No. But you and the boss don't want a firefight around the civilians, so that's the only other option."

"That's a fucking trap, Reaper," Brick hissed from beside him.

Kane knew it was, but while they were inside, maybe they could come up with a plan. "Zero, we're headed inside."

"Copy. All elements stand by."

———

Bull Horton sat in the black Mercedes SUV and watched Kane and the others turn and walk back toward the bank. Beside him in the passenger seat was Nicole. She said, "They know we're here."

Horton nodded in agreement. He reached down to grab his SIG P226 and said into his comms, "Blackbird Team go on my command."

"Wait," Nicole snapped. "What are they doing?"

Horton stopped what he was doing and watched. "They're going into the bank."

"They're continuing on mission," Nicole said, a hint of pride in her voice.

The Blackbird commander nodded. "He's a tough son of a bitch is Kane. I'll give him that."

"He's going after the ledger," Nicole said. "The other man with him was Falk. He's Marek's man."

Horton thought for a moment and then said, "Blackbird Four and Six, follow them into the bank but observe only."

They watched as their team members climbed from a white Mercedes and crossed the street. "Remember, observe only."

———

"Reaper One, you've got two tangos following you into the bank," Cara told him over their comms.

"Copy."

"Zero, what do you want us to do about these other assholes? Over," Cara asked.

"Just hold, Reaper Two."

"Copy." Then, "Axe, see if you can get an eye on who's in that SUV back there behind us."

"Yes, ma'am."

He leaned forward in his seat and rummaged around. Coming up holding a rifle scope, he turned around to look out through the back window, staying that way for a minute or so before turning back. He said, "I can make out two people in the SUV. One is Bull Horton himself, and the other is our friendly female CIA agent from the desert."

"Zero, these guys are Bull Horton's team. How do you suppose they found out where the hell we were?"

"No idea. But you can bet that if they're there, then Newcomb can't be far away. Keep alert."

―――――――

Inside the *Deutsche Bank der Schweiz*, Kane waited for Falk to open the box in the private room they'd been shown into. Brick stood near the door and waited just in case anyone chose to try and bust in on them.

Once the box was open, Falk reached in and retrieved the ledger. He passed it to Kane who flicked through it and smiled. "Bingo."

Stuffing it inside his shirt, he said, "Lock it up. It's time to leave."

Returning to the marble-floored foyer area, a line of customers waiting to be served, they looked across at the main entrance and the two armed guards who stood there holding SG 553s, both of whom had been there when they'd entered. The entrance itself doubled as a large scanner, sensing the presence of anyone entering with a weapon. The third guard sat at a desk, monitoring everyone coming through it, hence the reason that Kane and Brick weren't armed.

Then he spotted the two men from Bull Horton's team. The pair were huddled together a short distance from where they stood. Then he noticed something. Both were armed, the telltale bulges of handguns in their jackets.

"Brick, they've got guns."

"I saw them," he acknowledged. "Don't ask me how they got the things in here."

"They'll be plastic."

"Haven't those things been outlawed since the eighties?"

"CIA."

"You're right."

"Zero, we have a problem."

"Copy, Reaper."

"Our friends are armed with plastic guns. I need another way out."

"Wait, One."

There was a drawn-out pause, and then Thurston came over the comms. "Reaper One? Bravo. You've got three minutes."

Kane was confused. "How so, ma'am?"

"I just called in a possible terrorist alert. Three minutes is how long you have before the police get there."

"Copy, ma'am," Kane acknowledged. "The rest of you get that?"

"Copy," Cara said.

Thurston said, "They will be taken away for questioning for sure. What you need to do is shadow them and make sure that Horton's men don't try to intercept. If they do, you're clear to engage."

"Copy, Bravo," Cara said.

Now all they had to do was wait.

CHAPTER 18

THE SUN WAS JUST COMING up, and Paul Horn was on his way into work. He was speeding along the Georgetown Pike in his dark blue Chevy Suburban, wanting to get there early to monitor the op that was happening in Switzerland.

A few more minutes and he'd be at CIA headquarters. A few more –

"Shit, fuck!" Horn blurted out and swung hard left on the wheel of the Chevy, brakes coming on.

Before him, stopped dead in the middle of the road was a green Tahoe. Even if he'd jammed on his brakes and kept straight, he would more than likely have slammed into it, hence the left-hand swerve. And before he knew it, Horn was on Langley Fork Lane looking at another Tahoe the same color.

Horn came to a stop, cursing. He slammed the shift into reverse, realizing that something was wrong. The Chevy shot backward with a shudder of tires. He looked in the rearview mirror and saw the first vehicle pulling in behind him.

His foot hit the brake pedal again while his right hand made a dive for his personal weapon tucked inside his coat. By the time it was free, and his hand reached the door handle a man was already standing beside the driver's door with an M17 pointed at him. The man had operator stamped all over him.

A second man appeared on the other side and opened the door, an identical weapon in his hand. "This is a one-time deal, asshole. Get out of the car without any fuss, or I'll put a bullet in your fucking brain and walk away."

"Who are you?" Horn demanded.

The M17 centered on Horn's face, and he raised his left hand in a weak defensive gesture. "All right! All right!"

He opened the door and slid from the seat. The shooter on that side cable-tied his hands behind his back and put a hood over his head. Then they put him into the second Tahoe and drove away; his vehicle abandoned where it stood.

———

GENEVA, SWITZERLAND

Four SUVs pulled up out front of the bank, and ten men exited the vehicles. All were members of the *Groupe d'intervention de la police cantonale*. Geneva's special police unit within its Cantonal groups. They were dressed like special forces, which is what they were, in a way. They'd originally been formed to combat terrorism, like the rest of the Cantonal groups.

Each man was armed with a SIG SSG 553, the same

weapon as their famed Army Reconnaissance Detachment 10.

Two of the four SUVs had been parked to block the street one-hundred meters apart. Behind them were the Cantonal Police. The Cantons were another name for agencies, and Switzerland had twenty-six of them. All with their own police department.

Cara and the others watched them deploy. "These guys are good," Axe observed.

Cara nodded. "They sure are. I heard that they were trained by British SAS."

"Enough said."

"British SAS?" Arenas queried.

Axe said, "Tough motherfuckers who've kicked more bad guy ass than any other special forces group."

"Tougher than your Navy SEALs?"

"I'd hate to live off the difference. Back in World War Two, they used to drop them behind enemy lines before breakfast, and they'd have their mission tucked away by lunchtime. From North Africa to the streets of Ireland, and then into Iraq and Afghanistan. They've done it all. They even have special branches, depending on what's required."

"All right, enough of the history lesson," Cara said to them. "This shit is about to get real. Reaper One, you're about to have company."

———

"Christ!" Horton hissed through his teeth. "What the fuck is this?"

Nicole said, "Blackbird Base, are you seeing this? Over."

"Copy," the voice on the other end of the comms

replied. "They are responding to a report of someone suspicious looking going inside. It was made out to be a terrorist threat."

Shaking her head, Nicole said, "They're quick on their feet, I'll give them that."

Newcomb came on the net. "Everybody, hold your positions. If I'm reading this right, then the Cantonal police will take them out of the bank and transport them back to their HQ. Once they're mobile, we'll work out a place to intercept them."

They watched the police set up, and then as six of them moved in on the bank. Horton said, "Blackbird Four and Six, standby."

Long before the *Groupe d'intervention de la police cantonale* entered the bank, Kane had decided that he wasn't getting arrested. Too many variables, so he devised a plan on the run. It was pretty simple, really. The police were looking for a threat, and he'd give them one.

No sooner had the armed special police entered when Kane pointed at the two men from Horton's Blackbird team and shouted, *"Diese Männer haben Gewehre! Diese Männer haben Gewehre!"*

"What the fuck are you doing?" Brick hissed out of the corner of his mouth.

"I just told them that Horton's men were armed."

The policemen whirled and brought up their weapons, then started to shout at the surprised men who raised their hands above their shoulders. They were quickly restrained and relieved of their plastic, but lethal, weapons. Then the police laid them face-down on the cold marble floor.

While all the customers tried to gather themselves from the shock of the frantic action, Kane and the others slipped through the crowd and walked outside.

"What now?" Brick asked as he ran his gaze over the roadblocks set up at each end of the street.

Nodding toward an alley across the way, Kane said, "That way."

They moved briskly across the street, doing their best not to look suspicious. Off to their right, a police officer called out to them, trying to get their attention. "Keep moving," Kane said to Brick and Falk. Then into his comms, he said, "Reaper Two, abandon the vehicles. Bring what you can."

"Copy, Reaper One. We'll regroup on you."

The shouts from the local police grew louder, two of whom began to close the distance between them. Ferrero's voice came over the comms, "What are you doing, Reaper One?"

"Leaving," Kane told him. "Headed towards the river."

"That wasn't part of the plan, Reaper."

"Sorry, Luis, but the plan was fucked from the moment we arrived."

"*Stoppen! Stoppen!*" a policeman cried out in German. When that didn't work, he switched to French.

Meanwhile, Cara and the others had slipped from their SUV and were now cutting a straight line toward Kane's group. Out of sight inside their pants, they had tucked their M17s. And under their jackets were MP5SDs.

The team caught up with Kane before entering the alley and then they all disappeared.

———

Bull Horton was far from happy again. Twice he'd been made a fool of by Kane and his team, and he wasn't about to stand for it. "Blackbird One to Blackbird, copy?"

"Copy, Blackbird One."

"Permission to pursue on foot?"

"Permission granted, Bull. I want this ended today. You find them and kill them all. Finish it."

"Roger that," Horton growled and then he looked at Nicole. "Let's go."

He had three other men plus Nicole. The other two remained inside the bank. Five against five. As far as the Blackbird commander was concerned, the odds couldn't be more one-sided, in his favor.

His men were armed with CQBRs, and the sight of them all walking the street, loaded for bear took the policemen between them and the alley by surprise. On sighting them, the law enforcement officers immediately dropped their hands to their sidearms. A sharp whistle from Horton caused two of his men to raise their weapons and put well-placed bullets in their heads.

Then they too disappeared into the alley.

———

TEAM BRAVO WAREHOUSE, GENEVA, SWITZERLAND

"Christ! Did you see that?" Swift blurted out. "They just shot those policemen down cold."

A grim expression came over Ferrero's face. "Reaper One, copy?"

"Copy."

"You have a team of operators on your six. They just shot two policemen down near the mouth of the alley.

They number five in total, and one of them is a woman. Over."

"Copy, Zero. Rules of engagement?"

Thurston came on. "Reaper One, this is Bravo."

"Copy, Bravo."

"You will not engage. I say again, you will not engage. I don't want a damned firefight on the streets of Geneva. You escape and evade and find your way back here. Is that understood?"

"Yes, ma'am. But I'd like to point out that we may have no say in the matter."

"Then run faster, Gunny. Don't give them the chance."

"Copy, ma'am."

Thurston turned to face Ferrero who was staring at her. "What?"

The ex-DEA man walked off to one side, and the general followed him. Once they were out of earshot, he said, "I don't often question your decisions, Mary, but I think this is the wrong one."

Instead of getting mad at his second-guessing her decision, she said, "Tell me why and I'll consider it."

"You're hamstringing the team and putting other lives in danger, Mary. I know you think that the order you just gave is the right one, but it's not."

"Keep going."

"By not allowing them to fight, you are rendering them ineffective. Horton's men will have no such order, and you've seen what they are willing to do. They just shot two policemen without compunction. If we don't stop them, more innocent people will die. And they're not about to give up."

She stared at him for a time, and he could almost see

her thought processes whirring behind her eyes. Then
Thurston said, "OK, what do you suggest?"

"We lure them somewhere and take them all out at
once."

"What about the woman?"

"Her too."

"OK, Luis. Work on something. But just remember if
this all turns to shit, we're both screwed."

"Yes, ma'am."

Ferrero walked back over to where Swift was working
and said to him, "Find me a quiet place on the river where
the team can engage Horton's team without endangering
the local population."

"On it."

He turned and found Traynor and Reynolds watching
from afar. "You two gear up. Put your weapons and tactical
vests in the back of the third SUV. Then report back to me."

They hurried away, and Ferrero turned back to watch
Swift at work. "Have you got anything yet?"

"I'm good, Boss, but I'm not that good. But maybe
I am."

"Well?"

"The *Jardin Botanique*."

"English."

"The Botanical Gardens."

"Too many people," Ferrero snapped.

"A lot less than on the mean streets, Boss," Swift
pointed out.

"You could be right," Ferrero acknowledged. "Reaper
One? Zero, copy?"

"Copy, Zero."

"Make a left up ahead and head to the Geneva Botanical Gardens."

"Say again?"

"You heard me right. The Geneva Botanical Gardens. Make a stand there. And try not to kill any locals. I'm sending Pete and Brooke out to your location. Zero, out."

———

TEAM REAPER

"Did you all get that?" Kane asked them as they made their way along the street, trying to conceal their weapons as best they could. Kane had Cara's M17, and Brick had Axe's.

They replied in the affirmative that they'd heard the orders.

"OK, when we reach the gardens, we split up into teams of two. Cara take Axe, Brick and Me. Carlos, you take Falk and layup. Keep him and the ledger safe. Once Traynor and Reynolds get here, hand him over to them and tell them both to get the fuck out of here. The rest of us take out."

"Do you feel funny about this, Reaper?" Axe asked.

"Why?"

"They're our brothers in arms. Hell, we've both met him before, and all they're doing is following orders."

"It's them or us. We do what we have to survive. OK?"

"Roger that."

"All right, let's move it."

———

"This is it," said Kane. "Everyone check your comms. Bravo Four, copy?"

"Copy, Reaper One."

"Where are our friends?"

"They're about two minutes behind you. If I had to guess I'd say they're tracking you the same as we're tracking them."

"Can you shut them down?"

"I can try."

"Do it. Reaper One, out."

They entered through the main entrance; a grand affair made up of wrought-iron gates and stone pillars. The gravel path went on for ten meters before branching off in three directions. The first path hooked around to the left, through a variety of tall trees. The second almost traveled on straight away from them, while the third did a right hook towards what appeared to be a line of large conifers. Kane scanned the scene before him for civilians. There were a few scattered around that they could see, but most seemed to be off to the right where some parklands had been set out.

Then Kane saw what appeared to be a large glass greenhouse which looked more like an Indian temple. He pointed at it and said, "Carlos, in there."

"Roger that," he acknowledged and pushed Falk in that direction.

"Which way do you want to go?" Kane asked Cara.

"I've always had a thing for big trees," she said, nodding to their left. "We'll go this way."

"OK. If you come across any civilians, get them to leave the immediate area. Show them your gun if you have to."

"Copy. Good luck."

They took their leave and jogged away toward the trees, the gravel from the path crunching under their shoes. Kane turned to Brick. "Follow me."

Starting to walk briskly straight ahead, Kane called

into their HQ. "Bravo Four, how're you coming along with that blackout?"

"Almost there, Reaper."

"Hurry it up."

Kane and Brick followed the path as it banked around to the right and then deviated back left. It was lined with small shrubs and plants which were neatly manicured. A couple of larger specimen trees stood tall on their right as well, while to the left a small blank expanse of grass seemed incongruous with the setting, almost as though someone had forgotten to plant it out.

A dark-looking pond appeared ahead at their one o'clock. It was surrounded by thick reeds and a few sparse trees. Opposite was a narrow channel which weaved its way through rocks and tall grass. It was made to look swamp-like.

"Reaper, I've shut down their surveillance. The only problem is that they were using the same satellite as us. Which means we're blind too. Sorry, you're on your own."

"Copy, Bravo Four," Kane said. Then to Brick, "Just like being in the jungle all over again."

BLACKBIRD COMMAND, GENEVA

"Shit!" the computer tech hissed through clenched teeth.

"What the fuck just happened?" Newcomb demanded.

"They cut our feed."

"Who did? Thurston's lot?"

"Yes, sir."

"I don't care what it takes, get it the fuck back up, now."

The man's fingers flew across the keyboard as he tried to bring the feedback online. "Whoever locked us out is good, sir. It looks like that to do it; they also locked themselves out of the feed, too."

Newcomb nodded. "Blackbird One this is Blackbird Base, do you read? Over."

"Copy, Base."

"You're on your own, Bull. We've no eyes. The only bonus is that they don't have any either. But before we lost signal, they were splitting up. It looks like they're going to make a stand."

"I'm used to being on my own."

The comms went dead.

———

JARDIN BOTANIQUE, GENEVA

Bull Horton turned to his men and one woman. "Split up. They're making their stand here. Watch yourselves too. They've already made us bleed once."

Suddenly the squeal of tires drew their attention and two SUVs approached at a good pace. The Blackbird men brought up their CQBRs ready to fire. The vehicles shuddered to a halt and eight men climbed out, all armed with automatic weapons and dressed in tactical gear. Horton screwed his face up and asked, "Who the fuck are you?"

In heavily accented English, their leader said, "We work for Mr. Marek. We're here to help."

"The fuck you are," Horton swore. Then he spoke into his comms, "Blackbird Base, copy?"

"Copy."

The team leader reported what was happening and waited for a reply. Newcomb said, "Use them, Bull. Send them in first as a buffer for the rest of you."

"Copy. Blackbird One, out," Horton said grudgingly. "All Right. You want to help, then break your men up into teams of two and start helping. They're in there, somewhere."

The Marek team leader snapped a couple of orders, and his men split up and entered the gardens. Horton glanced at Nicole. He nodded at her handgun. "You want a CQBR instead of that?"

"I'll be fine."

"Suit yourself."

Cara watched as two men approached their position. She and Axe were laid up amongst some flowering shrubs where bees buzzed about their business, ignoring the presence of the two intruders.

She brought up her MP5SD, waiting for them to come nearer. "Let them get a little closer and then nail the bastards."

Unaware of their presence, the two men came on, eyes scanning left and right looking for threats. Cara knew that it wouldn't be long before the Geneva Police started to show, so was aware that they were running against the clock. The longer they lingered, and more sustained the shooting, it was highly likely that innocents would be killed.

Cara took a deep breath and said in a low voice, "Execute!"

She came to her full height and fired. The shooter on the left jerked under the impact of the rounds. He staggered and then fell. Beside her, Cara heard Axe's suppressed MP5SD cough twice and the second man crumpled.

Before moving into the open, Cara glanced around to check for further targets. When she was reasonably sure there were none, she said, "Let's get them under cover."

The pair hurried forward and grabbed the fallen men by their collars. Dragging them toward the shrubs, they didn't worry about the heels leaving furrows in the gravel path. Once they had them hidden, Cara did a quick dig through their pockets. When she found nothing, she looked for any distinguishing marks; again, nothing. Then she saw the weapons they were using. HK G36Cs.

"These guys aren't Blackbird, Axe," she said urgently. "Look at their weapons."

Axe turned from where he'd been keeping watch, and studied the carbines. "You're right. That means they can only be..."

"Marek's men or we've completely fucked up," Cara finished. She said into her mic, "Reaper One? Reaper Two, copy?"

"Copy."

"Reaper, we've got an issue. We just took down two men who aren't Blackbird."

"Say again, Reaper Two."

"I said they aren't Blackbird. My guess is that they work for Marek."

"Copy. Reaper One, out."

Cara looked at Axe. "Come on, let's move."

They broke away from their cover and moved further along the path to take up a new position.

Meanwhile Kane and Brick waited, watching from their position in the manmade swamp. Through the tall grass, they could see two men approaching. Like the ones who'd been killed by Cara and Axe, these guys showed all the marks of being military trained.

"You realize that once we open fire, we're going to draw shooters like flies to shit, don't you?" Brick commented.

"Easier to shoot that way," Kane retorted. "Saves us going looking. If we get a chance, once we put them down, see if we can get their weapons and ammo. I wouldn't mind a carbine about now."

They continued watching and waiting. Insects buzzed around Kane's head. He swatted at one of the little bastards just as it landed on his neck. *"Better than Colombia, Reaper."*

Chip's words rang inside his head. Kane tried to block his dead friend's words, and he whispered, "Not fucking likely."

"Say what?" Brick whispered.

"Nothing."

The pair of shooters were closer now, but Kane noticed something else. Coming along another path, on the other side of a small, reed-choked pond, was another pair of shooters. These two were different, however. They were armed with CQBRs. Kane said, "Over there, Brick. Two of Horton's men."

The ex-SEAL glanced over at the other duo as they walked along the path. "If we open fire on these two, those over there will hit our flank and have us pinned down."

"That's what I was thinking. Give me a couple of minutes to get into position. If I'm not ready when you are, then just open up, and I'll do my best."

"Where are you going, Reaper?"

"For a swim."

Kane snaked through the tall grass and into the water,

keeping himself low enough to be below the surrounds of the pond. It was cold, almost bone-chilling. He moved through the water and reeds slowly, trying not to get tangled. By the time he reached the other side, he was almost certain he was about to run out of time. He said into his comms, "In position Reaper Five."

"Ready when you are."

"OK. Three, two, one, Execute!"

Both men came erect. Brick from the tall grass and Kane on the slippery bottom of the pond.

The M17 in Kane's hand barked twice, and one of the two shooters on his side of the pond flailed around and dropped to the path. The second one brought up his CQBR and started to spray the area where the shots had come from before he'd even laid eyes on his target.

Lead hornets ripped through the air all around Kane, causing him to drop back down. The reeds were torn to shreds as the 5.56 rounds cut through them like a lawn-mower. He splashed to the left trying to escape the hail of gunfire.

Somewhere behind him, Kane heard Brick blow off a steady stream of fire. A shout told the team leader that at least one shot had hit a target.

Another burst of gunfire whipped through the reeds and Kane waited for a pause before he popped back up and fired three quick shots of his own.

One must have clipped the shooter because the man staggered. However, Kane was already dropping back down when he noticed it.

He paused and straightened once more. The shooter was down on one knee, a hand held to his chest, head bowed. One of Kane's shots must have hit him in the armor plate of his vest, stunning him.

Kane lurched out of the pond, a torrent of water

running from his clothes which could absorb no more. His boot slipped on the bank, and he had to put his left hand down to stop himself from falling. Cursing, Kane righted himself and brought up the SIG. He started to walk toward the hunched-over shooter, firing steadily as he went. Four bullets struck home, the last buried into the man's head.

Behind him, a flurry of gunshots sounded. Kane turned to see Brick shooting at the remaining man of the duo he'd been tasked to take down. The man fired a burst, and the ex-SEAL dropped out of sight, pinned down by the accurate shooting.

Kane turned and rushed across to the dead men he'd shot. He scooped one of the CQBRs and turned back. The carbine rose to his shoulder and the red dot sight centered on the killer. Squeezing the trigger and leaving his finger curled back, the team leader could see the bullet strikes and stopped firing. The man fell to the ground with a hole in his head.

With the gunfire ceased, Brick appeared. He looked over at Kane who signaled for the ex-SEAL to join him. Once he was there, Kane said, "Are you OK?"

"Yeah, I'm good."

"Get the other CQBR and any ammo."

The sound of sirens could be heard in the distance and Kane muttered a curse. The police would be here soon, and out there somewhere, Bull Horton still lurked. And God knew how many of Marek's men were left.

CHAPTER 19

SHENANDOAH NATIONAL PARK

IT WAS DARK, and he could hear voices. Somewhere between being taken and arriving at his destination, someone had jabbed him with a syringe. Now Horn was waking in a black fog.

In the distance there were voices. He strained to hear what they were saying but couldn't make it out. Horn's head hurt, and he guessed it was a side effect from the Ketamine he'd been given. If it was Ketamine.

The sound of a door opening and footsteps on boards, getting closer. Horn tried to move and found he couldn't. He was tied to something. Because he was sitting, he guessed a chair.

The person stopped beside him but whoever it was, said nothing. Instead, it was Horn who spoke. "You don't know what you have done by kidnapping me. You'll have people crawling up your ass so fast your head will spin."

Still, whoever was there remained silent. All the CIA

man could hear were the voices outside. Then the door opened, and a man spoke. "I can't believe you did this. I really can't. And now you've involved me in it."

A second man said, "This is all to do with national security. We need to know what they're up to. If they're willing to try and kill me, then who is next?"

"I don't like it."

"Well, it's done. Get the hood off him."

The hood came away, and Horn blinked, trying to adjust his vision to the light. The first person he saw was one of the men who'd taken him from his vehicle. He stared hard at him and snapped, "You won't get away with this, asshole."

"Shut up, Paul, you're in enough trouble as it is."

Horn shifted his gaze, and it settled on Frank Clavell, the speaker of the house. His eyes widened further when he saw Hank Jones. "What the fuck is this? Untie me right now. You two are both screwed over this."

Jones glanced at Hunt and nodded. The SEAL backhanded Horn across the face and stepped back.

Immediately, Horn tasted blood in his mouth as the inside of his cheek was sliced by his teeth. Clavell opened his mouth to protest, but before he could, Jones stepped forward and snarled, "Listen to me, asshole. You are so fucked right now; it's a wonder you can walk straight. So, let me tell you how this goes. We'll ask you questions, and you will answer them. Every time you refuse, our friend here is going to hit you. If that don't work, he'll start shooting you, and so on and so on. But don't think that he won't, because he will. This man has bled more blood for his country than you ever did. And right now, you and all your other conspirators are a threat to all he believes in. Understand?"

"Fuck you, Jones."

Hunt stepped in and landed a crunching blow to Horn's jaw. Not enough to knock him out, but sufficient to rattle him good and proper.

Jones said, "So to save on time, let me tell you what we already know. You sanctioned an illegal CIA op on American soil. That's bad right there, wouldn't you say, Mr. Speaker?"

"Yes, I'd have to agree there."

Jones continued. "And that illegal op was to kill a Pakistani reporter named, Hafeez Jiskani. Just plain murder it was. Because you found out that he was coming into the country and using the biker gang to get him in. That was why you had Newcomb, your best man, put your agent in there. That was so she could warn you when the time was right. But in the process, either she or Newcomb found out that we had a man in there too, so the son of a bitch burned him. It was just lucky that the rest of the team was on hand or he would have been dead."

Horn just stared straight ahead.

"So, you had Hafeez Jiskani killed because he had footage of a drone strike that went awry, killing thirty school children. But this is where things get a little mixed up. Why kill him? Air strikes have gone astray before. Then you put a termination order out on one of Thurston's team. Why?"

"Because he went off the reservation," Horn snapped.

"But then you try and have the rest of them killed. Even fly in Bull Horton's team especially for the job."

"How do you know?" Horn blurted out.

"I'm chairman of the joint chiefs. I have eyes and ears everywhere."

Horn went silent again.

"Let's break it down. We'll start with Jiskani. Why did you have him killed?"

No answer.

Whack!

"Why did you have him killed?"

No answer.

Hunt stepped forward again.

"Wait!" Horn said hurriedly.

"Talk," Jones snapped.

"Jiskani had to go because no one could look too deep at the missile that was used. It was a new experimental one from Black Shield. It was an unofficial test. The official test was meant to happen a week later at an undisclosed test site. But Drake and Forth couldn't wait. They wanted it tested yesterday. When it all went south, the trial was pulled so the issues could be fixed. I sent a cleanup crew into the area to make it all go away. It was then that we found out about Jiskani taking the video. The missile had several obvious components which were different and if something survived the explosion and was caught on the feed, then it couldn't be seen."

Jones snorted. "The thing is, the video you got, the one he was killed for, wasn't the only one. Our tech did some digging and found another. It must have been a copy. So, you killed him for nothing."

"Shit."

"Yes, shit. Now, what about the team?"

Horn looked at both men. "Before I go on, I want a deal."

"That depends on what you give us. You could tell us first, and we'll consider your request, or I can get my man to beat the shit out of you, and we'll get it that way. Make your choice."

Another sigh came from Horn. "The connection was made that if news of the missile got out, then Poland wouldn't go through with the missile defense contract. It wasn't until after the negotiations had started that we found out about his other activities."

"Wow, the CIA fucked up. That would be a first," Clavell's voice dripped with sarcasm.

"Keep going," Jones snapped.

"Anyhow, Drake wasn't about to back out of the deal. It was worth too much. He offered me ten million to keep it quiet. And Forth wanted the deal to go ahead because he'd set it up, and if it all went south, he could say goodbye to the Whitehouse. Then that stupid kid of Marek's dropped a tab in that girl's drink, and she died. From then on it was a matter of trying to keep it all quiet. But your boy wouldn't let it go."

"And you issued a termination order against him."

"Yeah, but I can't figure out how you knew that," Horn allowed. "Then the rest of your team showed up in Europe. By then, Marek had sent his son to Latvia. I can only gather that your people went after the lab and came across the kid by mistake."

Jones looked over at Clavell. "Is that enough for you?"

The speaker nodded. "It is. For now. We'll get him back to Washington, and the FBI can take over."

"What about my deal?"

"You'll have to work that out with them. Just be thankful that Hank didn't shoot you."

"There's something else. Forth knows that you know, and he was planning something for you."

"I'll take care of that," Clavell told him.

"What about the men who came after me?" Jones said. "Did we get them all?"

Horn shook his head. "There is a man the CIA uses. I'll give you his name."

"Make sure you do. Let's get out of here."

———

JARDIN BOTANIQUE, GENEVA

The temperature in the greenhouse was equivalent of that of a South American jungle. Hot, humid, and the scent of damp earth hung heavily in the air. Arenas was crouched amongst the green leafy plants of the exhibit while he waited for the all clear. He'd been monitoring the chatter on his comms and knew that there were now two teams of shooters out there instead of just one.

Beside him, Falk sat patiently, showing no sign of fear. Under his arm was tucked the ledger.

The greenhouse was deserted and had been since the arrival of Arenas and Falk. One look at the weapon the Mexican was carrying, and people seemed to melt into thin air. He heard the door to the greenhouse open and knew that it could only be the ones they were hiding from. He flicked the fire selector on the MP5SD around onto burst. Then he waited.

The sound of muffled footfalls told Arenas they were close. He peered through the foliage and caught sight of two men. Arenas eased himself back and used hand signals to motion for Falk to get down.

He was about to raise his MP5 into the firing position when the growth around him disintegrated in a hail of gunfire.

"*Puta!*" Arenas cursed out loud and dropped to the moist ground beneath him.

Falk shouted as he did the same, and at first, the

Mexican thought the man had been shot. His head whipped around, and he caught sight of the drug manufacturer trying to scramble away through the undergrowth. Arenas reached out and through brute strength dragged him back.

Falk turned and stared at him, eyes wide. The Mexican glared at him and growled, "Stay the fuck there, asshole."

Then Arenas turned and disappeared through the shredded greenery.

———

Kane and Brick edged their way through the plants and shrubs which were densely grouped together. The rattle of gunfire sounded from the direction of the greenhouse, and then more erupted from somewhere behind them.

"Sounds like this thing is really starting to kick off," Brick said.

Kane nodded. "Reaper Two? Reaper One, copy?"

"Copy, Reaper One."

"Sitrep, over?"

"Four tangos down, over."

"Copy. Reaper One out," Kane said. Then, "Reaper Three, sitrep?"

Nothing.

"Reaper Three, sitrep?"

The channel opened, and through the sound of gunfire, Kane could hear Arenas' voice. "Give me a minute, Reaper."

"Hang on, Carlos, we're coming to you," Kane snapped. He glanced at Brick and said, "Come on, let's go."

They broke cover and began to sprint in the direction of the greenhouse. It was a stupid move, and against everything, the former recon marine had been taught and practiced over many years. And they ran straight into trouble.

"Hold it right there, asshole!" Horton snapped. "Didn't being a recon marine teach you anything?"

Kane and Brick halted and turned to see Horton, Nicole, and another operator standing on the path. "Guess we missed them," Brick said.

————

Arenas ducked back behind a large brown rock as bullets hammered into it, sending shards slicing through the air. Another burst cut through the foliage and a branch dropped to the Mexican's left. He muttered something in Spanish as he slapped home a magazine and loaded a round into the chamber.

Leaning around the rock, he let loose with a sustained burst of fire and saw one of the shooters buckle at the knees. Ducking back, Arenas waited for the firing from the remaining shooter to cease before once more exposing himself.

This time, however, he appeared on the other side of the rock and took the shooter unawares. The MP5SD ripped slugs across the man's torso, knocking him back. Taking a step forward, Arenas fired again, and this time the bullets tore a gaping wound in the killer's throat.

Arenas whirled and pushed back into the man-made jungle where he found Falk, still laying where he'd been told to stay. The Mexican said, "Come on. It's time to go."

————

Kane stared at the three people standing before him. In the distance, he could hear the police sirens growing louder as they came closer. Bull Horton had a satisfied expression on his face which Kane took to mean that they were both about to die. Beside the Blackbird commander stood Nicole, armed and silent.

"I see we meet again," Kane said to her. "I guess it was bound to happen. Laying down with dogs and all that."

"Not the way I wanted it," she said.

Kane shifted his gaze to Horton. "I see you're down a few men, Bull."

"All good they were too."

"Now they're dead," Brick joined in. "I guess you picked the wrong team to go after."

"I'm about to correct that."

"Even if you do," Kane said, "there's still more than enough out there to take you down. Watch out for the woman. She'll kill you quick."

A cold smile touched Horton's lips. "You won't see it."

Sirens grew louder as the police cars neared.

"You'd better hurry up then, asshole. I'm sick of waiting."

"Hold it!" Brick snapped.

Everyone stared in his direction. Horton frowned. "Why?"

Brick said, "This is your last chance to get out of this alive, Horton. If you try to kill us, then you'll die. All three of you."

The Blackbird commander snorted derisively. "Fuck off."

The ex-SEAL shrugged. "You were warned."

Horton moved to fire, and as he did, the sound of suppressed gunfire slapped at the air. Horton and the last remaining Blackbird operator jerked wildly, and bullets hammered into them. Beside the dancing pair, Nicole spasmed as she took her own rounds and slumped to the ground.

It was over in seconds. The three lay side-by-side and Kane hurried forward to check them. From behind a round shrub, two figures appeared. Traynor and Reynolds. The DEA man said, "Glad we made it in time, I was beginning to think we wouldn't, the way Brooke drives."

"Oh, shut up, you're in one piece."

He smiled. "Are you all OK?"

Brick nodded. "Just."

Kane looked up and said, "Get the others to regroup on us. We need to get the hell out of here before the police are breathing down our necks. Brick, stay on me. Gather what spare ammo these guys have. This isn't over."

"Copy."

Kane knelt beside Nicole. The woman was still alive but not for much longer. Blood flowed from the bullet holes in her torso and from the corner of her mouth. She was having trouble breathing, and from the rattle deep in her chest, he guessed her lungs were filling with blood. Her eyes fixed on him, and he said, "Sorry about this but it was bound to end badly."

She gave him a weak smile, revealing blood-stained teeth.

"Where is he? Where's Newcomb?"

Nicole shook her head and struggled to raise her hand. It tracked toward the inside of her coat. However, the agent's hand fell short, weak from blood loss. She looked at Kane with pleading eyes. "Inside...pocket."

Kane reached in and found what she was looking for. He placed it in her hand and then asked again, "Where's Newcomb?"

"House...river," Nicole managed and then died. Her

hand fell to her side, and she dropped what she'd been holding.

It was a blood-stained picture of a little girl. "Fuck it," Kane muttered.

The team leader came to his feet and took a couple of spare mags that Brick offered him. The ex-Seal said, "What now, Reaper?"

Kane's gaze hardened. "We finish this fucking thing. Come on."

"I'm with you," Brick said.

As they hurried away from the scene of the shooting, Kane said into his comms, "Bravo Four, copy?"

"Copy, Reaper One."

"Newcomb is set up in a house on the river somewhere. I need you to pin down his location somehow. Can you do it?"

"I can try."

"That's all I ask. Send me his location when you do."

"Copy."

"Reaper One, this is Bravo, copy?"

"Go ahead, Bravo."

"What are your intentions, Reaper?" Thurston asked.

"I'm going after Newcomb," Kane informed her. "Apart from the ones that the police got, Blackbird Team is down, so are those who belong to Marek. Also, you can add Nicole to that list."

Kane paused and then added, "She had a little girl."

All Thurston said was, "Good luck, Reaper."

"Ma'am."

They regrouped with the rest of the team and Falk, then made their way toward the vehicle driven there by Brooke. They hid their weapons in the back and put Falk in there with them. When he started to protest, Kane gave him a withering glare which soon shut him up.

The team were about to climb in when Swift came back over the comms. "I found your man, Reaper. I'll send the address through to you."

"Thanks, Slick. I owe you a beer."

Kane looked at Cara and said, "Let's go kill this asshole."

CHAPTER 20

"SIR! We've lost contact with Blackbird Team. I can't raise them at all."

Newcomb frowned. "What about Nicole?"

"She's not answering either."

"Shit," Newcomb swore. "How long since you last had contact with them?"

"Thirty minutes."

The CIA man just about exploded. "And you're only just bringing this to my attention now? How fucking stupid are you! Put everyone we have left, on alert and start packing up. Christ!"

Suddenly an alarm sounded from a laptop and another tech turned, a perplexed look on his face. "They've found us."

"Who?"

"Them," he said pointing at his screen.

Newcomb went around to look and saw what the tech

saw. He took out his personal firearm and said, "Evacuate, now. Tell the others we've got trouble."

By others, Newcomb meant the handful of CIA operatives that he'd brought with him to act as security for their operations center. There were only four of them because that was all he'd thought he'd require. Hell, he hadn't expected them to get past Horton. What a fuck up.

——————

The double-story house was old and rundown. The garden was overgrown, and the grass in the yard was almost knee high. Tiles were coming off the pitched roof, and one of the gates hung off its hinges. But what gave away the presence of something else were the small CCTV cameras sited in areas where they could cover all approaches. When Kane saw the first one, he said to his team, "Once we pass this point, they'll know we're coming. Anything with a weapon is fair game. Press forward and get it done. If you see Newcomb, don't hesitate. Put him down. Axe and I will take the front, Cara, you take Brick around the back. Carlos, watch our man here. Pete and Brooke, watch the perimeter."

"Roger that."

The team moved swiftly through the gates and separated into their pairs on the other side. Kane and Axe hurried toward the front door. He paused at the foot of the steps. "Reaper Two, sitrep?"

"Give me twenty seconds, Reaper."

"Cover our six, Axe," Kane said and mentally counted the time off. By the time he reached fifteen, Cara came back over the comms. "Reaper Two in position."

Kane paused another heartbeat and said, "Execute! Execute! Execute!"

He kicked open the front door and stepped around to the left just as a wild, hailstorm of 5.56 rounds filled the void. Axe had stepped to the right, so he too was out of the firing line.

The muzzle of the shooter's weapon shifted, and the wall around Axe seemed to explode outwards in a phalanx of wood splinters. "Motherfucker!"

Kane leaned around the doorjamb and fired the acquired CQBR. Unlike their normally suppressed HK416s, the CQBR roared to life. Bullets streaked across the space to find a home in the man's chest. He dropped to the floor and Kane breached.

The team leader swept the room, looking for more threats. Behind him, Axe swept left and rear to make sure no one was closing from behind. Kane pushed forward and heard the flat slaps of a suppressed firearm coming from along the hallway that led toward the rear of the building. They were followed by the crash of an unsuppressed weapon, additional suppressed, and then a shout of pain when at least one round burned home.

The next thing, Cara and Brick appeared coming along the hallway toward them. Using hand signals, Kane directed them to move onto the stairs and clear the second floor. He and Axe would clear the first.

They crossed the dirt-strewn floor to the first door which was slightly ajar. They burst through the opening and swept the room. It was empty, so they moved on to the next one. It too was empty apart from cluttered, dusty furniture. The next room, however, had signs it had been used. Unlike the others, this room was cleaner and still had all its electronic gadgets inside. A knot of electrical cables ran across the floor and into the wall. Kane glanced at the nearest monitor and saw that it was hooked to the

CCTV cameras, showing multiple angles of the house's exterior as well as the perimeter.

Then Kane saw it. One of the cameras was showing a darkened area which looked like another hallway. Axe said, "They left in a hurry. Must've got out once they saw us outside the perimeter."

"Yes, and I know where they've gone," Kane told him. Then he said into his comms, "Reaper Two, copy?"

"Copy."

"We're clear down here. How's it looking up there?"

"Nothing but dust, dirt, and pigeon shit."

"Copy. Meet me at the bottom of the stairs."

"Roger."

"On me, Axe."

"Coming, Reaper."

Kane headed for the door. "Zero? Copy?"

"Copy, Reaper One."

"The bird has flown, Zero. Have Slick run a search of the perimeter to see what he can pick up. They went underground. For a rundown dump, I'd say the CIA have used it before."

"Roger, I'll get him onto it. Zero, out."

The others joined them at the foot of the stairs, and Kane said, "They've gone underground. We need to find out where they went. Everyone pick a door and be careful of what might be behind it.

They split up, and it was Brick who found what they were looking for. The doorway led to a staircase which dropped away into a lit passage. Brick took point, followed by Kane, then Cara, and the last man down was Axe. The lit passage ran west for around twenty meters before turning north.

"Bravo Four, copy?"

Static.

"Bravo Four, copy?"

Nothing.

"Bravo One, copy?"

Nothing still.

"Damned comms are out," Kane cursed. "Brick, keep moving."

They pushed along the underground passage for another fifty meters before it turned once more, opening out into a larger room filled with crates. "What do we have here?" Brick said with a low whistle.

Kane said, "Axe, Cara, crack a few of these things to see what's in them. Brick, on me."

The two of them walked along another tunnel until it stopped at the foot of a ladder. At the top of it was a two-door opening with only one hatch open. Kane led the way up the ladder, and when he emerged, he was in a stand of trees, about ten meters away from the river, its steep embankment dropping five meters to the water. Kane said, "I bet that's how they got the crates in."

"It's probably how they escaped too," Axe added.

"Bravo Four? Reaper One. Copy?"

"Copy, Reaper One."

"Any luck?"

"Not a damned thing."

"The tunnel came out on the river. I think that was the way they escaped. We found some crates in a storage room. Reaper Two and Four are checking them over as we speak."

"Copy. I'll tell Zero."

"Come on, Axe. Let's see what the others found."

They went back down the ladder and into the tunnel. From there they trekked to the crate storage room. "What have you got?"

"You won't believe this shit," Cara said. "We've got

money and weapons. A quick calculation in my head puts it at somewhere between five and ten million dollars."

"CIA stash?" Kane proposed.

"Could be. Whose ever it is, they're not going to be happy about losing it."

"I'll call it in, and Thurston can deal with it. Get the team mobile. It's time we left."

———

TEAM BRAVO WAREHOUSE, GENEVA, SWITZERLAND

"We're out of here within the hour," Thurston told the team gathered before her.

"Where to, ma'am?" Brick asked.

"Home. We're wrapping things up."

"There's still things to be done here," Kane pointed out.

The general nodded. "Not for us. We have the ledger, and it will be passed on to the proper people in Poland. I talked to General Jones, and he says that Horn is willing to testify against Jim Forth and Mark Newcomb."

"Providing that they can find him."

"Ken Drake is also in custody. The FBI picked him up this morning their time."

"What about the money and weapons in the house?" Cara asked.

"What money? The general is sending people to pick it up. The money will be put somewhere safe, and we'll be able to call on it when required. Call it our war chest."

"I sure would still like to have nailed Marek," Brick said.

"He'll get his," Ferrero told him. "There's too much evidence against him."

Thurston's cell rang. She took it from her pocket, hit answer, and said, "Thurston."

She listened to the person on the other end, all the while under the constant gaze of her team. After a minute or so she said, "Thank you," and then hung up.

"What is it?" Kane asked. He'd seen that concerned look before.

"Marek gave the Polish authorities the slip. He's in the wind."

"Fuck it," Axe growled.

"He'll turn up," Thurston said. "They always do. And when he does, we'll be there to get him. But for now, let's get packed up. We've got a plane to catch."

CHAPTER 21

KARMA BEACH CLUB, INDONESIA—ONE MONTH LATER

THE SUN WAS STARTING to set, and the sky was beautiful with red and purple streaks. The couple sat at the bamboo bar, drinking Tequila Sunrises and smiling at each other. The bar itself sat on the sand under an awning constructed of a framework of bamboo poles along with a grass and bamboo thatch. The structure's supports too were mostly bamboo; thick trunks fixed together to make everything sturdy.

Other couples sat at tables in Balinese chairs, talking, drinking, enjoying what would turn out to be a warm evening. Banana lounges were placed further out on the beach where tourists could sit and watch the slap of the clear-blue waters against the tropical sands.

Set to the right of the small beach was a large screen, set to show one of the latest movies after dark. Behind it was the lush rainforest which framed everything it surrounded.

The couple at the bar ordered another drink. The woman wore a white bikini top and a sarong around her slim waist. The man wore blue shorts and a T-shirt. Off to their right, a man approached the bar, dressed in shorts and a floral shirt. He walked past them and found a seat that he frequented every day at that time. Sitting down, he waited for the waiter to come and take his order.

The woman elbowed the man who turned to look at the new arrival. She said, "Looks like he's been getting himself a tan."

"I hope he's been enjoying it because it's all about to stop. Let's go and say hi."

They rose from their seats, taking their drinks with them. Walking across to where the man was seated, they joined him without invitation. A flare of recognition flickered through his eyes, and he gave a wry smile.

"Well, well. If it isn't the Reaper," Newcomb said, making the name sound derogatory. "To what do I owe the pleasure?"

"You're a hard man to track down," Kane said. "But we managed."

The ex-CIA man nodded. After the incident in Europe, he'd been disavowed. As he'd fully expected, but he was good at his tradecraft and was sure that no one would find him here living under his new identity. "So, what now? I'm to be arrested? I picked Indonesia for a reason. No extradition treaty, remember?"

"There is that," Cara allowed. "But we just thought that after we went through all of the trouble to find you, then maybe you'd just give up and come in of your own volition?"

Newcomb chuckled, his confidence obvious. He'd not been greasing the hands of officials in the local government for the past month for nothing. "I don't think so. I quite like it here. The weather is nice. The view is spectacular, and tonight they are showing one of my all-time favorite movies, The Sound of Music."

Kane shrugged. "I guess we had to ask."

"You've asked, now go away."

Kane and Cara climbed to their feet and turned to walk away. Then, as an afterthought, Reaper turned back. "Did you know she had a daughter?"

Newcomb was confused by the question. "Who?"

"Nicole. She had a little girl."

"Of course, I knew. But that's part of the job. She died. It happens."

And that was it.

Kane and Cara walked away along the beach, the clean sands squishing up between their toes. Newcomb watched them go, a cold smile evident on his face. He reached forward and picked up his newly-arrived drink.

Cara said, "He's an asshole."

"He is," agreed Kane. Then he said, "All yours, Reaper Four."

Axe's voice filled Kane's ear. "Sending."

The 7.62mm projectile whistled out of the jungle at almost eight-hundred meters per second. It blew through the back of Newcomb's chair, into his torso, and then out through his chest in a spray of blood. He grunted and looked down at the blood splatter on the glass he held, confused. Then his eyes traveled further to look at the rapidly-spreading patch of red staining his shirt and shorts.

Newcomb looked up, having one final glimpse of the ocean as the light inside his eyes started to fade. Then his head slumped forward, and he dropped the glass to the sand beside him.

"Target down."

Cara said, "I guess Karma is a beach after all."

———

TEAM REAPER HQ, EL PASO, TEXAS

Thurston and Ferrero stared at the slumped form on the screen before them. The general said, "Well, at least he got his."

Ferrero nodded. "Any news on Marek?"

"Not yet. The NSA are keeping tabs on all his known contacts. Sooner or later he'll reach out. And when he does, they'll get him."

"Let's hope so. I hate leaving loose ends. Especially ones that can come back to bite us on the ass."

Thurston sighed. "Me too. Make sure Reaper and the others get on that plane. I want them stateside within forty-eight hours."

"Another job?" Ferrero asked.

"There's always another job."

"Yes, ma'am."

———

LOS ANGELES, CALIFORNIA—ONE WEEK LATER

"I should have been there for her, Reaper. I let her down."

Kane stared down at the headstone with the name Remy Burton etched in gold lettering at the top. "You couldn't have known, Axe. None of this was your fault."

"It don't feel that way."

Kane nodded. "It'll get better. You know it will."

"Yeah. But I don't want it to just yet. She was a good kid."

The cell in Kane's pocket buzzed. He reached in and took it out. It was a message from Ferrero. Axe looked at him and asked, "We gotta go?"

The team leader nodded. "Sorry. Take your time. I'll go over to the SUV and wait."

"No, it's good. I'll come now."

Kane patted him on the shoulder and indicated the headstone. "I think the boss did good, huh?"

Axe nodded. "Yeah. Remy would have liked that."

A LOOK AT: BLOOD RUSH
A TEAM REAPER THRILLER

A RACE AGAINST TIME. A BATTLE ACROSS BORDERS.

Kane and his elite crew face their deadliest mission yet. After capturing Jorge Sanchez, the ruthless leader of the Chologos drug cartel, a new threat emerges—his daughter, Blanca. Determined to free her father, Blanca takes hostages and plants a bomb in a New Jersey school, setting the stage for a global showdown.

For three relentless months, Team Reaper has pursued Sanchez across the world. Now, with their reputation on the line and innocent lives in the balance, they must stop Blanca before the Chologos cartel rises again.

Inspired by real-world events, including the infamous El Chapo trial and the rise of cartel heirs, *Blood Rush* delivers explosive action straight from today's headlines.

Will Kane and his team stop the Chologos cartel for good? Find out in this pulse-pounding installment!

AVAILABLE NOW

ABOUT THE AUTHOR

A relative newcomer to the world of writing, Brent Towns self-published his first book in 2015. Last Stand in Sanctuary took him two years to write. His first hardcover book, a Black Horse Western, was published the following year.

Since then, he has written twenty-six western stories, including some in collaboration with British western author, Ben Bridges; several action adventure novels, such as his bestselling Team Reaper series; the novelization to the 2019 movie, Bill Tilghman and the Outlaws; as well as scripted a handful of Commando Comics. Not bad for an Australian author, he thinks.

Often up until the small hours of the night, bashing away at his tortured keyboard in Queensland, Australia, Brent loves to lose himself in the world of fiction. If you're interested in sharing your thoughts in more detail, scan the QR code below! Your feedback is invaluable to him—and often helps shape his future writing endeavors.